OF TALES AND ENIGMAS

OF TALES AND ENIGMAS

MINSOO KANG

PRIME BOOKS

OF TALES AND ENIGMAS

PUBLICATION HISTORY: "Lady Faraway," "The Well of Dreams," "The Dilemma of the King and the Beggar," all appeared in *Lady Churchill's Rosebud Wristlet* 11, 2002; and "Gyeongbok Palace: History, Controvery, Geomancy" in *Manoa* 11 (2), 1999. All other stories are original to this collection.

Prime Books
www.prime-books.com

CONTENTS

My deepest gratitude goes to Jeff VanderMeer, of course, not only for this but for everything, beginning with the solution to the numerical tale. Thanks also to Professors Robert Rosenstone, Mauricio Mazon, and Michael Heim for their continued support and understanding. Fond regards to my willing and unwilling audience over the last years, Adam Barnhart, Megan Barnhart, Chris Bates, Jeff Blutinger, Rebecca Casey, Dan Crosby, Lawrence Culver, Ron Davidson, Jay Fisher, Kimberly Garmoe, Fiona Halloran, Sara Hendren, Kyung Moon Hwang, Soo Yun Kang, Susanna Lim, Ken Little, Mark Pollard, Courtenay Raia, Lars Schumacher, Gabriel Wolfenstein, and Hillary Zifkin. And special thanks to Nikos Gnoma, the greatest deceiver, Sun Inho, the darkest enigma, and Penelope Rienzi, the loveliest muse.

I. TALES FROM A LOST HISTORY

FOUR TALES AND AN ENIGMA

When I think of the mystery of that winter night, it is not the event itself that disturb me so much as the way I remember it. I can recall every detail of those hours as if it all happened yesterday—the scene, the actors, and the brief but amazing encounter that aroused our imagination, as well as every word of the stories we then exchanged. Yet I have no recollection of how I came to be at the place or how I departed from it, as the memory stands in my mind like a short tale in the middle of an otherwise blank volume. What is most troubling is that while I can clearly picture my companions of the night, I have no idea who they were or what became of them.

My recollection begins with us, five in number, in the cramped but clean hall of a rural inn, celebrating over a banquet of fowl, fish and lukewarm beer. I cannot tell you what we were celebrating or why we were celebrating it in that particular place, but the occasion was a merry one as we sat by a well-lit fireplace and feasted, all of us talking too loudly, laughing too much, and consuming too many pitchers of beer. The innkeeper was happy enough to serve us at first but soon tired of our antics and sat sulking at a corner table, waiting for us to finally retire to our rooms. Yet we only demanded more food and drinks throughout the night as we joked, played games, and sang without a thought to the passing time.

The inevitable hour arrived when we began to feel the weight of fatigue and overfull stomachs, and our merriment gave way to the languid melancholy of revelry's end. As our conversation slowed down and then faded into silence, we sat morosely, each of us waiting for someone else to suggest that we call it a night. The innkeeper dozed at his table; Tristan checked his watch and continued to stare at it with a puzzled expression as if he could make no sense of it; Grey drank slowly from his mug, allowing a thin stream of beer to trickle down from the corner of his mouth; Cyrus sat with a thoughtful expression, his eyes empty and his arms crossed tightly over his chest; and Nikos began to tell us something about love but then forgot what he was going to say in mid sentence and snickered at himself. I myself yawned and had to blink my eyes several times to clear away the tears. When I could focus them again, my attention was drawn to the hall's main door which slowly opened with a quiet but sharp creak. We all turned then and beheld what would captivate us far into the night.

A short elderly gentleman in a dark overcoat walked cautiously into the room, followed by a young woman in a lace dress and thin cloak. The former was a thoroughly repulsive looking fellow with a ridiculously bulging belly and the thick features of a toad. On his enormous head, crowned by sparse but wildly dancing gray hair, tiny dark eyes darted to and fro above flaring nostrils, a protruding lower lip and two doughy folds beneath his chin. His short but thick limbs and quick, nervous movements made him look like an overfed reptile. He was attired, however, in clothes of the finest cut, the fur-lined coat, the silk scarf around his bulbous neck, the glistening leather boots and the velvet hat in his gloved hands all marking him as a man of means.

The woman, on the other hand, captivated us at once with her extraordinary beauty. Everything about her was pale and fragile, from her slender figure to her perfectly oval face that featured large, luminous eyes, thin nose and lips, and exquisitely curving cheek bones beneath a skin that was so white that it was almost blue. Her long hair was tied severely behind her lean neck and reached down to her waist. She walked closely behind the gentleman with her head bowed and her hands folded before her, not casting us a glance.

As we watched in fascination, the couple approached the innkeeper who promptly awoke and got to his feet before making a quick bow as if he had been expecting them. After he led them up the stairs, we waited until the sounds of their footsteps faded down the corridor before turning to one another and falling into a suddenly frantic discussion of the extraordinary newcomers. Fatigue and drunkenness fled from us as we talked excitedly, offering all manners of observations. As our conversation quickly became confused, we decided to hold an impromptu story contest in which each of us would, in turn, tell a tale of the strangers.

"The most striking as well as mysterious thing about them is the young lady's apparent subservience to the gentleman," the ever impatient Tristan declared first. "You saw how she followed him closely like an obedient child, not daring to even look in our direction. But what is the nature of his power over her? Is it paternal, avuncular? I think not, for there is not even a hint of a resemblance between the two. Is she then his employee? Then why is she dressed like a lady? I believe that the solution to the mystery lies precisely in the incongruity of her manner and her attire, for it was obvious that she is not used to wearing such finery. Her awkwardness in those clothes gave her the appearance of a dressed-up doll, and that is what I think she must be, a plaything of the gentleman.

"Imagine, then, a rich and powerful aristocrat of, let us say, monstrous tastes, who makes monthly journeys from his rural estate to the city to indulge his perversions. With his enormous wealth he has no trouble finding discreet and pliant ladies of the night for that purpose. Over time, however, his needs become increasingly elaborate and bizarre, until one night, he goes too far and seriously injures two women, rendering them permanently unfit for their profession.

The abused ladies appeal to their other rich and powerful clients, and the gentleman is forced to hand over a substantial sum in order to avoid prosecution. He is, furthermore, forbidden to set foot in that city again. He leaves the place humiliated and enraged.

"On the return journey to his estate, his coach passes by a procession of vagabonds, peasants who have lost their lands to a flood and are now destitute. The gentleman notices among them a young girl in tattered clothes trudging exhaustedly behind her parents. She is emaciated and covered in filth, but he sees with his connoisseur's eyes her hidden beauty, so perfect to his taste. He orders his man to turn the coach around.

"'You there,' he addresses her parents who look up in astonishment.

"'Is that girl there your child?'

"'Why, yes sir, she is,' the father answers uncertainly. 'She is our one and only daughter.'

"'I am in need of a maid at my place and your girl will do. What say you to her entering my service?'

"The bewildered parents look at each other, not knowing what to make of the sudden offer. The gentleman frowns in annoyance at their hesitation and takes out a purse of coins.

"'Of course you ought to receive something for it,' he says and pours the money out onto the muddy ground.

"The parents stare at the shining things for a moment before they rush to pick them up. Other starving peasants run to their side also, frantically pushing and grabbing at the coins. In the confusion, the gentleman signals to his man who seizes the girl and easily lifts her into the coach. As the vehicle pulls away from the malodorous mass of people and speeds down the road, the screaming girl is pulled down by her new master who grasps her throat, choking off her cry.

"'If you want to live, you will be quiet and do as I say,' he threatens her.

"He lets her go only when he is sure that she is frightened enough to obey him. They travel to the next town where he takes her to a bordello and has the women there clean her up and put her in a fine dress so that she will not draw attention for the rest of the journey. As it is already late when she is finally made ready, the gentleman decides to spend the night at a discreet inn at the edge of the town, at this very place. He won't touch her tonight, as he will wait until he has her securely in his domain before practicing his abominable pleasures at leisure."

Tristan concluded with a mischievous smile and drank some beer.

"What an awful story!" I exclaimed.

"Terrible!" Grey agreed with me. "How could you think of such a thing?"

"Oh, spare me your indignation," Tristan answered irritably. "You must have had such a thought yourself. There she was, a beautiful young girl, following that awful man like a frightened dog."

"But why does the fellow have to be so perverse?" Grey demanded.

"Obviously to draw sympathy for the girl," Nikos answered for Tristan. "Come now, it was an effective device. The more heinous the villain, the greater our concern for the lady in distress."

"Is it really sympathy though," Cyrus put in, "or desire masked as sympathy? Perhaps another reason the gentleman has to be monstrous is this legitimizes our desire to take his place."

"Because the story makes us want to rescue the girl from him?" Nikos asked.

"More than that. What is even more troubling than her plight is the reflection in it of our own lust. Who among us would not like to have such a beautiful creature in his power? The villain disturbs us because we recognize a part of ourselves in him."

We reflected on that for a moment before Grey responded.

"Well, I admit to the girl being desirable to me," he said. "I even confess to finding something provocative in the fellow's power over her, but I question the unnecessary nastiness of the story. I can imagine an entirely different explanation of his power over her."

"Then you should tell us of it," I suggested.

As the others turned to Grey, he took a moment to gather his thoughts before starting.

"Tristan was struck by the girl's subservience to the fellow," he began, "but my attention was drawn primarily to the young woman herself. Did you not see that there was something unearthly about her? Her beauty was like that of an apparition. Passing us for but a moment, she managed to captivate us all, despite our varying tastes. So I believe that there must be something otherworldly about her identity and her relationship with the gentleman.

"I picture then a warlock of great power, living alone in his hermetic keep, studying and experimenting in order to learn the language of creation. After spending half his life wresting precious but all too few secrets from reluctant Nature, he realizes that he cannot possibly complete his work in his lifetime. What he requires is an assistant who is as able in the mysterious art as he. As no human person can fulfill that role, the warlock decides to seek help from the supernatural realm.

"He uses his arcane knowledge to construct a magical portal to another world, and opens it to find beyond a spirit in the form of a beautiful young girl who looks at him with astonishment.

"'Who are you?' the innocent creature asks.

"'The master of the world on this side,' he tells her.

"'What is your world like?'

"'Full of wonders light and dark, fair and foul. Come through here and I will show it to you.'

"'But I belong here, in this world,' she says uncertainly.

"'Nothing will happen if you visit for a moment.'

"The spirit thinks over the offer. 'All right,' she says, 'but you mustn't keep me long since I have to return home presently.'

"As soon as she steps through the threshold, the warlock slams the portal shut and secures it with a magic lock. He then shows her the one and only key.

"'Without this you will never return to your world. You will be stuck in this one where all is heavy and mortal. But if you work as my assistant for ten years and work well, I will grant you this key.'

"The spirit weeps and begs him to let her go, but he is unmoved by her entreaties. She finally realizes that she has no choice but to obey, and becomes his student.

"In the following years the warlock makes great progress in his work thanks to his supernatural subaltern. He does not know, however, that when he sleeps, the spirit steals into his library and studies his books, to learn the makings of a magic portal. With only a year left to her service, she finally acquires the knowledge, goes down to the deepest part of the keep at midnight, and fashions a gate into another world. When she opens it, however, she discovers, not her own gentle and ethereal world, but a fiery place full of mad demons. The twisted creatures spy her and rush through the gate before she can close it. She screams in terror as the demons scatter through the keep, destroying everything in sight. The warlock awakes at the tumult and sees what she has done. He battles the demons and eventually manages to hurl them back through the portal, but not before the creatures have ravaged his house, incinerating his books and reducing the place to a smoking ruin.

"'You fool!' the warlock bitterly reprimands his assistant. 'Did you think that you could return home merely by creating another portal? As if yours is the only other world! Did you not know that there are an infinite number of worlds? You have done me good service in the last nine years and I would have freed you after one more, but now, because of your foolishness, all my work is destroyed. I must go forth from this place and find a new home, there to repeat all my studies. And you will come with me, reckless one, and help me regain everything that you have caused to be lost, and not until then will I release you.'

"And so the warlock and the spirit leave the devastated place in the guise of an elderly gentleman and a young lady. They come to this inn, where they will rest for a night before continuing their search for a new home."

"Ha!" Tristan exclaimed. "You were supposed to provide an explanation of who they are, but you tell us a fairy tale instead."

"What is wrong with that?" I asked.

"It is an easy way out," he answered. "Do not misunderstand me, I enjoyed the story. But warlocks and spirits aside, those were actual people we saw. Grey's tale does not tell us anything real about them."

"But when did we decide that our stories had to be realistic?" Nikos asked. "All we agreed on was to tell the best story we could of who they are. If he chose to tell one of the fantastic, then that was his right."

"I am not disputing his right to do so," Tristan said. "What I am saying is that the story had nothing to do with the truth about those people."

"Is that what we are doing?" Cyrus questioned. "Searching after truth?"

"Like the warlock himself!" Grey said cheerfully before taking a sip of beer.

"Oh, I see," Nikos said and gave out a short laugh. "The story was really about us and our little contest. We are the warlock, you see. And in our search for truth, we summon our stories as he summoned the spirit."

"But she caused everything to be destroyed," I pointed out.

"As our tales may lead us further away from what we are seeking," Cyrus put in.

"But with a story that has no connection to reality," Tristan said, "we are left with but a dream."

"We have the stories," Cyrus said.

"But what use are they?" Tristan questioned.

"It's not a matter of use. Think of them as allegories."

"Allegories of what?" I asked.

"Of our wonder," Cyrus said. "And I have an allegory of my own, if I may be allowed to present it next."

"By all means," I said and we all turned to him.

"As contrasting as the previous stories were," he began, "they shared in an unwarranted assumption about the relationship between the two guests. What makes you so certain that she is in the inferior position? Because she followed the man? But servants and bodyguards commonly precede their masters. Because of her bowed head and modest manner? Coyness is often used as a disguise and a bait. I do not believe that she is a slave or a spirit at all. I believe that she is quite human, but monstrously so.

"Whether through possession by a malevolent spirit or some dreadful disease of the mind, the creature brings calamity to all those around her. Only when she has disappeared will people realize that what they took to be a series of chance misfortunes in her family was the direct work of the monster. Pity will then turn to horror as they shudder at the infamy of her progress.

"For the first ten years of her life, she is the only and much adored child of a wealthy landowner and his wife. During that time, she gives no outward sign of being anything but an ordinary child, a little spoiled perhaps and given to surprisingly elaborate pranks that reduce the maids and governesses to tears, but nothing to indicate what she will become. The only incident that gives pause to some involves her puppy, which was thought to have run away until it was found dead in some woods not far from the estate. A few days before the dog disappeared, the family went on an outing during which the girl saw a handsome Great Dane in a nearby village. The girl asked her father for such a dog but was refused, as she already had a pet. But with the mysterious demise of the puppy, she received the dog of her desire as a consolation.

"It is with the birth of her little brother that the shadow of evil falls fully upon the house. The boy is born healthy and becomes the new darling of the house, but after only a few months of bringing joy to the family, he dies inexplicably in his sleep. The mother falls into a deep depression, spending her days sobbing in bed and hardly venturing out of her chamber. Then the little girl's governess, who always looked on her pupil with suspicion, falls from a balcony on the third floor and breaks her neck. When questioned, the girl says that she slipped while leaning over the railing. A few years later, just when the mother is finally recovering, her daughter pays her a visit, during which the former becomes hysterical, screaming, tearing her hair out, and scratching her own face. Her husband is forced to put her in an asylum, and is left with only his daughter and the servants in the great mansion. Its residents lead quiet and anxious lives, fearful of reawakening whatever has wreaked such havoc upon this once happy family.

"After the girl turns sixteen, her father arranges a marriage for her. The groom is a younger son of another wealthy landowner, a decent enough fellow but quite lackluster. After the wedding ceremony, the newlyweds embark on their honeymoon, during which a freak accident occurs, the husband falls out of their carriage and plunges down a cliff. The young widow returns to the house of her father.

"A year later, the servants hear a gun discharge in the master's office where they find him at his desk, his head shattered by a bullet. He has left a note on his desk that reads, 'For my sins against my daughter which have returned to me a hundredfold.'

"A few more years pass, and the now wealthy widow takes on another husband, this time a handsome dandy from a noble family. They attend the most fashionable social functions, apparently very much in love. After only a year of marital bliss, however, the husband begins haunting his old playgrounds again, sometimes spending days away from his wife, in the company of harlots and drunkards. He then suddenly falls ill, and dies after a few days.

"Within a year, the twice-widowed lady takes on yet another husband who also dies under mysterious circumstances. Following this incident, members of her deceased husbands' families become suspicious and persuade a local prosecutor to inquire into her affairs. After a preliminary investigation, the official, accompanied by constables, goes to her estate in order to question her directly. When they arrive at the mansion, they find the place empty. They discover that she dissolved her assets into liquid cash before dismissing all the servants except a certain elderly fellow who acted as her personal assistant. She then disappeared without a trace.

"There are rumors that she and her man go about in the guise of a wealthy gentleman and a modest young lady in order to entice young men in out of the way places. She attracts them not only by means of her considerable beauty, but also by appealing to their chivalrous nature, as someone in need of rescue. When a man accosts her, she plays with him for a time before doing away with him with the help of the servant. Some say that she does it for sport, in the spirit of the hunt, while others say that she is compelled by vengeance, from some deep hatred of all mankind."

"Well, that is another thoroughly unpleasant tale," I said.

"And another vicious lunatic!" Grey exclaimed. "I would like to know why you are driven to make such monsters out of them."

"Perhaps because their mystery is so monstrous," Nikos suggested.

"What do you mean?" I asked.

"They have done something to us. Just by seeing them once we have become slaves to their image. And as much as we may have appreciated the lady's beauty or enjoyed these stories that we tell one another, none of us likes being enthralled like this. I consider Cyrus's tale both a retaliation against our captors and an indictment of our susceptibility."

"A retaliation," Tristan said, "because it attempts to dissolve our fascination by demystifying them. To make monsters out of them, as Grey put it, in order to shatter our illusions."

"And an indictment," I said, "because questioning our assumption about the girl's subservience reveals our naiveté, our fatuous idealization of beauty. We are perfect victims of their diabolic game!"

"But for what purpose?" Grey asked. "Look, we are never going to find out the truth about these people, so why pretend that some stories are more real than others? What if the tale does disillusion and demystify? Where does that get us? All we are left with is a feeling of dread in a void of ignorance."

"So you think that we should tell more fairy tales?" Tristan asked.

"That is not his point," Nikos said. "Why should we restrict ourselves to mundane explanations when we are just inventing stories? I also think that Grey ought to be offended by the last tale."

"Why is that?" Cyrus asked in concern.

"Although Grey was horrified by Tristan's tale, he acknowledged its insight into the role of power and took account of it in his story. You, on the other hand, ignored Grey's acute observation that there was something uncanny about the young woman. As instructive as your story was in overturning our assumption about the relationship between the gentleman and the lady, it was uninformed by the previous tale. In telling my own story, I should be obliged to keep in mind all your observations."

He took a sip of beer and began his story.

"I also imagine a seeker after knowledge, like Grey's warlock, but not at all powerful or ambitious. He is, in fact, a mad, aging vagabond who wanders from town to town. Although he has long ago forgotten what he seeks, he is driven by a desperate need to find that secret thing his soul yearns for.

"One day, he is overcome by fatigue and lies on the ground, falling into a deep, death-like sleep. When he awakes, he finds himself on the loneliest shore, in the saddest land, on the darkest night of the year. Unable to bear the prospect of continuing his fruitless search for a forgotten object, he decides to throw himself into the ocean to drown. As he makes his way to the water's edge, he sees something flickering on the sand and stops to examine it. He finds a small mirror lying just beyond the reach of the water, the image of a beautiful young woman on its glimmering surface.

"'Who are you?' he asks her.

"'I am a cloud goddess who is trapped in this mirror, on this loneliest shore in the saddest land.'

"'Who put you there?'

"'The great god of lightening and thunder.'

"'Why did he do this to you?'

"'Because he wanted to possess me, to flash and bellow from inside me, but I refused him.'

"'Why did you refuse him?'

"'Because I wanted to turn into gentle rain, to shed my tears upon the saddest land and quench its thirst.'

"'Will you be trapped in that mirror forever?'

"'The benevolent goddess of the rainbow took pity on me and promised that on the darkest night of the year a man without memory would come to ask me three questions. Answering the first would free me from this mirror. Answering the second would free me from this loneliest shore, and answering the third would free me from this saddest land, and allow me to roam the sky once more.'

"'Who am I?' the vagabond asks.

"'You are the man who loved the most beautiful woman in the world.'

"With that answer, the young woman springs from the mirror and appears before him in all her divine splendor. She waits for him to ask the next question, but he sits down on the sand and gazes out to sea, contemplating the stream of his slowly returning memories. He remains there, letting the days and nights go by, watching the great body of water undulate before him, uttering not a word. The cloud goddess stays with him and brings him food and pearls from the sea, hoping to move him. But he remains silent for an entire year.

"When the darkest night of the year arrives again, he suddenly asks his second question.

"'What am I searching for?'

"'You are searching for your beloved, the most beautiful woman in the world.'

"Next morning, she takes him out of the loneliest shore in the saddest land and to the nearest town, where, with the pearls she gathered, she arranges the most comfortable life for him, putting him in a house with all the luxuries. He spends another year in silence, locked in his remembrance. When the darkest night of the year arrives once more, he asks the cloud goddess the final question.

"'How can I be with my beloved again?'

"'By following me to my destination,' she answers him.

"Next day, she packs up their belongings and orders a coach. They leave the saddest land and embark on a journey that takes another year, finally arriving at this inn. They will stay here for a night, but then set off in the early morning to arrive at the great mountain over there, on the darkest night of the year. She will take him up to its highest peak where she will finally turn back into a cloud goddess and bear him up into the sky. When she has ascended as high as she can fly, she will let him go and watch him plunge into a crevasse of the mountain, where many years ago the most beautiful woman in the world fell to her death, causing her lover to go mad and become a vagabond without memory."

We sat in silence for a moment, contemplating the tale.

"So the lady's manner was not that of modesty," Tristan said, "but sadness at what she will do."

"This is the first tale in which the gentleman is the victim," I pointed out.

"But can he be called that?" Grey questioned. "She is only taking him where he means to go."

"A victim of fate then," Cyrus answered.

"It makes me wonder at our depiction of him in the previous stories," Tristan said. "How we maligned the fellow!"

"His unabashed ugliness," I suggested, "but also our envy of his connection with a beautiful woman."

"What slaves we still are to outward appearance," Cyrus said.

"But to an inward desire as well," I said.

"Surely not for her?" Grey questioned. "Not after the last two tales."

"No," I answered. "I am thinking of a desire of a more abstract nature. The desire for a solution to our uncertainties. The desire symbolized by our search, through our stories, for the truth about the mysterious couple. But a story doesn't necessarily have to contain a solution. It can be an enigma in itself."

"So you will tell us an enigma instead of a story?" Cyrus asked.

"Yes, but not the kind that you may be expecting. I enjoyed all your stories, but I have always had a penchant for enigmas. In mine, I imagine five storytellers, the best of friends, who are celebrating at a rural inn. I cannot tell you what they are celebrating or why they are celebrating it in that particular place but it is quite a merry occasion as they joke, play games and sing late into the night. When they finally tire and think of turning in, the door opens and they see

☯

There my memory of the night comes to an abrupt end. I cannot, therefore, tell you who won the contest or how he was rewarded. Nor do I recall how we finally departed from one another's company. There is, however, a small ensuing fragment of memory, which is an even greater mystery to me. So strange a bit of remembrance is it that it may well be from a dream I had that night. And yet this story, or enigma, would be incomplete without it, as it provides a conclusion of a sort.

I was in my room, I remember, lying in bed and staring out the window on the opposite wall, watching the blue of the night turn gray with the arrival of the new day. Despite my fatigue, I found myself unable to fall asleep, the tales we had told and the image of the people who inspired them swirling in my mind. Feeling restless beneath the heavy blankets, I decided to go outside and watch the sun rise. I got up and dressed, putting on a heavy coat and gloves in anticipation of the morning chill.

I stepped out of the inn, into a cold, fog-filled world, and breathed in the sharp freshness of the dew-laced air. After stretching my arms and letting out a mighty yawn, I gazed out at the countryside, until I saw the gentleman and the lady standing by the side of the dirt road that ran just outside the inn. Stunned by the unexpected encounter, I stared at the pair, who stood perfectly still, like dark figures in an obscure painting. A moment later, a coach clattered out of the morning fog and came to a stop before them. The gentleman swiftly opened the door and helped the lady climb in before lifting his plump body into the vehicle. He paused for a moment then and looked impassively around the area, as if inspecting an insignificant part of his vast empire. He gazed at the round hills barely visible in the distance, the desolate fields all around us, the modest inn's aged brick walls, and the road ahead stretching into the mist-veiled distance. He did not see me standing there, frozen in wonder, as he finally pulled himself into the coach and closed the door behind him. The coachman took up the reins and the horses began to move forward.

I must tell you that it was an extremely foggy morning, and I would not take offence at the suggestion that the combined effects of fatigue, alcohol, and an overactive imagination could have played a trick on my mind. Yet in the fresh silence of that dawn, I would have sworn by everything that was holy to me that as the carriage moved onto the road, it disappeared into thin air right before my eyes.

THE KING AND THE STATUE

The King ruled in an age when the power of the monarch was absolute, and the island state that was his realm was famed for the exotic beauty of its women, as it is to this day. So it has always been a mystery to me that he could not find one he saw fit to be his queen. According to the story, he became disgusted by the licentious behavior of certain women of the place, who may have become the first prostitutes in history through a curse brought down on them by a deity for some unspeakable crime, and that ever since he regarded every woman with suspicion and dissatisfaction. And so, the great poet wrote, he chose to sleep alone at night. This displeasure, whether from an extraordinarily finicky nature or an innate revulsion toward the feminine, is assumed to be the cause of that fantastic event that made him both a legend and an archetype throughout the ages, namely, his mad love for the statue of his own creation.

But if one seriously considers how a man could feel a passion for an inert image of a woman that he could not for a living one (a truly bizarre thing, after all, since the agonizing softness of the flesh, the ephemeral glances of desire, and the melodious whispers in the ear are some of the finest attractions of a real woman), the cause may be revealed as the effect, and the effect, the cause. In other words, perhaps it was a preexisting penchant for beauty in a still, inanimate form that made him indifferent to the living, that caused him to think at a certain time: 'How fair that servant girl over there is. How flawless her golden skin, how radiant the tresses of her copper hair, how elegant the lines of her trim shape. If only she would not move so, if only she would be still. Why does she have to ruin it all with motion, with change, with life? As beauteous as she is in stillness, she is becoming always. Becoming new, becoming old, becoming another. One day she will grow ugly with age, die, and rot, just as I will also age, die, and rot. All that I have will be lost to me in this world where everything is changing all the time. Why cannot all be still and remain still, in a moment of perfect peace? I feel ill and grieved. A curse on that servant girl. Once again, I will sleep alone tonight.'

Yet the longing for stability and immortality can only be a partial explanation for the desire for the inert and the immutable. What he felt for the statue, the story makes quite clear, was a profound visceral passion that one cannot expect from something that merely brings peace. The King was clearly in love with the thing itself, but it was not enough for him to simply gaze, caress and even lie with it. He desired it to come alive, but not, I believe, so that it might simply become a living woman like the others in his realm whom he found so unsatisfactory. What he wanted was a lover who embodied the best attributes of both a statue and a woman, someone who was concrete and unchanging but also capable of responding to his desire and acting upon her own. Of course it was an impossible thing he wanted, which is why, as the story recounts, he had to resort to supernatural means to achieve his end.

If his love for the statue was indeed the result of a predisposition rather than a discontentment, his negative attitude toward living women being a mere side effect of the former, how did he come to harbor such a singular passion? While it would be easy to consider it a strange quirk of an inborn nature, I believe it is much more fruitful to speculate on a single defining moment of his life when the desire came upon him as a powerful transforming force.

The richly fertile island that was his home lay like the glistening lips of a full, welcoming mouth in the middle of the well traveled sea, between the sun-drenched empire of the old race in the southern continent and the perpetually quarrelling city states of the new in the northern. Its people were ethnically, linguistically, and culturally of the northerners, but due to its position as the center of trade between the two races, they accepted the ways of the southerners to a greater extent than any of their mainland cousins. Traditionally, the old race was the more civilized people, as the history of its vast and powerful empire, filled with wonders that made foreign visitors doubt their own senses, stretched back far beyond the time northerners first began to scribble down accounts of their own meager doings. The dark-skinned people, therefore, were regarded as more intelligent and refined by nature, but also more effete and calculating, while the pale inhabitants of the north were considered brutish and naive but courageous in battle. The term 'new race' itself originates from the time an emperor first brought the northerners in as mercenaries to strengthen the ranks of his army during the great conquest of the desert, and was used pejoratively by the southerners for what was barbaric and crude. The official imperial chronicle tells of a general who subdued a rebellious city and was in a hurry to march on to the next, so he neglected to arrange a proper ritual of victory to the gods. A venerable priestess chided him by saying, 'I see that you have taken on the ways of the new race, Sir General. Strife and blood first, reverence and decorum last.' The General blushed in shame and delayed the march to make amends.

The people of the island were eager students of the ways of the old race. Travelers have noted how they had adopted many elements of imperial manners, attire, and learning, and how their art and architecture featured interesting combination of southern and northern styles. Most citizens were bilingual, and many apparently of mixed blood as well, which accounted for the exotic beauty of their women. They prided themselves on being the intermediaries between the two races and profited much from that role as the island thrived on economic and cultural trade.

By the time the King was born, however, the empire of the old race was crumbling and the fortune of the new on the rise. As the rule of imperial law weakened in the time of the Succession War of the Five Princes, commanders of the southern fleet took to raiding northern merchant vessels. The archons of coastal city states sent a joint envoy to the empire, asking its immortal ruler to put an end to the piracy by punishing his renegade admirals. The heroic poems chronicling the conflict that followed claim that the ambassadors were treated with contempt and dismissed without satisfaction, but a reliable memoir of a high imperial minister recounts how it was explained to the northerners that his master was unable to grant their request at the moment since all military resources were being put to quelling the revolt of the Emperor's brothers and half-brothers. The envoys were sent back, the minister claims, not only with a promise of justice at the conclusion of the war but also with some treasures as partial payment for the losses incurred at sea. When the diplomats reported on the chaotic state of the south to their archons, they saw a great opportunity. The rulers of the new race set aside their differences to form the Northern League and organized a great expeditionary fleet, ostensibly to protect their merchant ships but with the true purpose of invading the empire.

The King was still a youth when he witnessed the conflict between his father, the Crown Prince, and his grandfather, the reigning king, over the question of joining the League. The old man on the throne, who was besotted with love for his teenaged concubine, a southern girl from an aristocratic family, ruled that the island state should side with the empire, which would surely reward them for the loyalty when stability returned to it, and not join their uncouth cousins in some foolhardy war that would bring nothing but calamity on them. His son, who despised him and his lover for having driven his mother to an early grave with their affair, organized a coup with those who disagreed with the King's policy. A cowardly misstep by one of the conspirators nearly caused the plan to go awry and an outright civil war to break out, but the Prince's men managed to capture the train of the concubine as she tried to flee the city. The two sides were preparing to do battle in the streets when the Prince asked for safe passage to meet with his father. When the latter agreed, his son came to his palace with only a handful of his most loyal men, walked up to him in the audience chamber and cast the head of his concubine onto the stone floor. The King lost heart at the sight and surrendered to his son. After he abdicated from the throne, the new ruler of the island immediately sent an envoy to the mainland to join the League. Within weeks, his warships sailed as a part of the expeditionary fleet.

Endless squabbles among themselves had made the northerners masters not only of warfare, but also of diplomacy and treachery. They made alliances with some of the rebellious imperial princes, then betrayed them when they had outgrown their usefulness. They maneuvered the factions of the southerners into fighting one another until they all became exhausted, unable to defend themselves against the onslaughts of the invaders. In less than five years, the major armies of the imperials were crushed, the Emperor had fled to the farthest provinces of the endless desert, and the coastal lands of the continent had become colonies of the new race.

In the final months of the war, the young prince of the island accompanied his father to a city on the coast that was to be ruled with the brother of the King as its governor. It was one of the most ancient cities of the fallen empire, full of wondrous structures and other marvels. And it was there that the impressionable youth first saw the statue of his desire. As he rode beside his father through the awesome sights of the great polis, surrounded by bodyguards whose armor shimmered brilliantly in the southern sun, his attention was drawn to the lofty statue of a female deity, standing tall and unscathed on a high pillar, above a great pile of stones from a demolished wall. He stared at the graceful form with a serene expression on the flawless face and the arms extended in invitation to an embrace, knowing that he had never seen anything so beautiful in his life.

I must mention at this point that according to art historians the island was a great center of the arts, boasting a rich tradition in mural painting, but it knew little of sculpture-making at the time, as the few stone and clay products that predate the period are rather crude in nature. There is a story told in an imperial collection of literary and artistic anecdotes of a famed southern animator, which is what sculptors were called in the empire, who had traveled to the island state a century or so before the war. There, he created works that were lifelike to a degree never seen before in the place, with the faces full of expression, limbs extended and bodies in mid-motion poses. Those who came to see them were both amazed and terrified, and soon rumors spread throughout the city that the sculptor was a sorcerer who could actually bring his creations to life. After more tales began to circulate of how the statues left his house at night and walked the streets to cause mischief, a mob came to destroy the uncanny works. Once they were all reduced to rubble, the furious sculptor left the island, but the people continued to report sightings of walking statues in the dark. The tale is most certainly apocryphal since historical and archaeological evidence show that the island already possessed a sophisticated artistic and intellectual culture at that time, unlike the more backward inland cities of the north where such a superstitious belief could easily take hold. I am willing to entertain the idea, however, that the superior sculptural art of the old race may have contributed to the young prince's amazement at the sight of the goddess. But that does not explain the enormity of its effect on him, how it transformed him utterly in a single moment, and how the mad love he would foster for it would make him the subject of an enduring fable.

That night, as the young prince slept in the vast and strangely built chamber of a marble palace, he dreamt of the goddess who came to him in a cloak of blinding light, embraced him, and made him her ardent lover. When he awoke, he found that he had spilled his manly seed in great profusion in the night. During his remaining days in the city, he kept a lookout for that statue but he never came across it again, though he went everywhere with his father as he toured the ancient city.

The father and son returned to the island; years passed in peace; the father died; and the son ascended to the throne. On his first night as the new king, he dreamt again of that goddess, and she returned to him periodically in the first years of his reign, slowly building the fire of his obsession until his mind began to turn molten from its heat. And perhaps it was this image of the ideal feminine that caused him to find the women on the island worthless, as he steadfastly refused to take a queen from among them. Then news arrived that his uncle, the governor of the ancient city, was dying, which gave the King an opportunity to return to the place, not only to appoint a new governor but also to seek the image of his ecstatic and torturous dreams.

When he arrived at the colonial city, his uncle was breathing his last, but managed to recommend as his successor a protégé of his, an able administrator who was of mixed blood. The King duly made the appointment, presided over the ceremonies, and finally went through the funeral rites for his uncle. Once his official duties were done, he set about looking for the statue, only to be met with a perplexing mystery. Inquiries into the source of the serene-faced, open-armed image revealed that it was that of the city's former patron goddess. When the city had been conquered, the deity's priests had been given a choice by the King's father to either enact an official ceremony for the citizens in which it would be announced that the goddess has freely chosen to become a concubine of the island's god of the sea and storms, or face utter annihilation with their temples burnt to the ground, holy images destroyed, and worshippers slaughtered. The priests had taken the first option and told the faithful a story of how the goddess had submitted herself to the northern god for love, and the god had taken her into his benevolent embrace before commanding that her people be ruled by his, and that they should live in peace. The citizens of the city, however, had understood the true nature of the tale and had abandoned their worship of the goddess altogether, for they had seen no reason to continue their reverence for a deity that failed to protect them from being conquered by barbarians. Her temples had become empty as even the priests had eventually given up on their faith and left the place. By the time the King returned to the city, there were only three priests who remained true to the goddess, one who was too old to change his ways, another who was simpleminded and knew no better, and the last who was mad and believed himself to be a half-mortal son of the deity.

The King questioned the old priest, and was confounded to learn that there was no representation of the goddess, in painting or in sculpture, as that was explicitly forbidden by the religion. Instead, they had always worshipped the image of a firebird, her holy creature, which was to be found everywhere in the city. When the King told him that he had seen the statue of her as a young man, the priest was astonished and claimed that it was a vision of the goddess herself. He then took him to a square behind the central temple, which the monarch recognized as the very place where he had seen her. There was the pillar upon which the statue had stood, at the base of which was a damaged sculpture of a firebird which had fallen from the height.

"A wall stood there, my Lord," the priest informed the King, "which was leveled by your father's men after the archers who guarded it were brought down. The day after you first came to this city, the firebird fell from the pillar in the night. Your father ordered it to be left there, as a sign and a symbol."

"But why would your goddess reveal herself to me," the King asked, "when I did not even know of her existence before that day? And why should she appear in my dreams, to embrace and to love me?"

"It appears, my Lord, that she left our people to be with you, wherever you go."

"But why me?"

"Why do we love those we do, my Lord? Why them and not others? Perhaps the mystery of your vision and your dreams is the mystery of love."

The King thought deeply on the matter during his remaining days in the city. When it came time for him to depart, he ordered the old priest to accompany him, leaving the central temple under the charge of the simpleton and the madman. He also took with him some of the best animator-sculptors of the city. The first thing he did upon his return was to build a temple to the goddess, on the outskirts of the city and modest in size so that the priests of the island's sea and storm god would not be too offended, and put the old priest in charge of the place. He then set the sculptors to work on making images of the goddess, according to the recollection of his vision. His palace became filled with the sounds of their hammering and dust from cut stones.

When the first batch of their works was done, the King viewed them but found none of them to his satisfaction as they all seemed only to be crude approximations of his desire. Countless more attempts to satisfy his demands also ended in utter failures in his eyes. The frustrated King considered executing the incompetent artists, but another dream of the goddess in the night gave him an inspired idea. He dismissed all the sculptors and sent them back to the ancient city except for the best among them, who was made his teacher in the art.

☯

It should be of no surprise that the pursuit of this obsession made him neglect his kingly duties. He became oblivious to the events in the world and to those in his own realm that would bring about his downfall. The Northern League was falling apart as the archons of the new race fell to fighting one another again, in the north and in their southern colonies as well. The mad priest of the ancient city, who thought himself the son of the goddess, gained the trust of the governor and began to convince him that he was the true heir of the old emperors who was destined to rid the land of the barbarians and rebuild the empire. And on the island itself, the richest merchants gathered regularly in secret meetings, hatching a plot to reduce the monarchy to a figurehead position and establish an oligarchy. The King's most loyal advisors and ministers tried to draw his attention to such developments, but he spent all of his days perfecting the craft of statue making.

One day, after he had put the finishing touches on an ivory statue and stepped back to examine his creation, he saw that he had finally achieved his purpose. Before him stood that grand deity of the serene face and open arms, beckoning him to her embrace. It was the very image that he had seen as a young man.

"This is it," the King said. "It is her. I have done it. I have brought her back to me."

"It is a perfect statue, my Lord," his teacher said in amazement of his royal student's work. "It is greater than anything I have ever made, or hope to make. You have nothing more to learn from me, my Lord."

The King dismissed him with a handsome reward and sent him back to the ancient city. He then stood before the statue for days, staring at its still form, caressing its shape, and kissing its cold, hard flesh. He whispered to it, embrace it in nakedness, and lay with it at night, loving it as he had never loved anything in his life.

"Yet you do not know my love," he said to the statue. "You do not know the agony I suffer for you, this fire that burns within me, this longing that is like a bottomless well. You cannot know, you cannot know me, because you are still, you are unchanging, you are perfect."

He fell to his knees before it and wept through a deep, dark night. When he had no more tears to shed, he was overcome by exhaustion and slept at the statue's feet. He dreamt of the goddess again, but woke up to find her still inert. As he could not bear the sight of her any longer, he left the chamber to clean himself. He then ventured out of his palace for the first time in years and walked through the streets of the city that was, unbeknownst to him, no longer under his control. He made his way to the temple of the goddess where he found the old priest lying ill in his bed.

"I made her," the King told him. "I did it. But it was not enough. She still came to me in a dream. She is still not with me in life. What must I do? How can I bring her to me at last?"

The priest was gathering his strength to answer him when another voice came in the darkness. "Our ancestors knew the secret of animating a statue by bringing a spirit into it, my Lord. That is why our sculptors are called animators. It became forbidden because it is a dangerous art, for spirits who were forced into statues against their will became wrathful creatures that wreaked havoc, and sometimes evil demons freely entered them for their own diabolical ends."

"Is the art lost then?" the King asked the darkness.

"It was, my Lord, but no longer," the voice said. The mad priest from the ancient city, who had stolen into the island to spy on its state, emerged from the darkness bearing a scroll.

"You!" the old priest said in horror. "It is you, the mad one. And you have found the forbidden scroll. How do you dare? How do you dare bring it here to risk the damnation of . . . "

His words were interrupted by a blade in the mad priest's hand that swiftly cut his throat.

"Does that scroll contain the secrets of the art?" the King asked desperately, hardly noticing the murder of the old priest committed before him.

"Yes, my Lord."

"Then you must give it to me."

"As you command, my Lord. But before I do, I must ask a favor."

"Anything."

"Once you have used the knowledge to bring the statue to life, you must burn the scroll, so that others may not practice this dangerous art."

"I will do so, I swear to you."

In the course of the events that followed, however, the King must have forgotten his oath as there is no record of his destroying the scroll. That gave rise to many legends in the centuries to come about the fate of the forbidden writing, how it fell into the hands of various sorcerers and madmen, how they created animated statues of stone and clay, and how some of the creatures turned against their creators and became monsters. Even today, the so-called 'Book of Animation' or 'Unholy Book of the Ancient Animators of the Old Race' makes its appearance every once in a while in horror novels and movies.

The King took the scroll from the mad priest and returned to his palace to find a group of merchants and military commanders, who had been bribed into supporting their cause, waiting for him. With bowed heads, they humbly begged him to examine and approve a document they had put together which they called a declaration of their loyalty to the monarchy and the state. While the writing affirmed their absolute submission to the King, it cleverly took away all real power from him, or rather 'relieved him of the burden of everyday rule that his obedient subjects may humbly bear.' As the King was anxious to go to his statue, he gave it only a cursory reading before putting his seal on it.

While loyalist ministers and commanders were being imprisoned and murdered by the soldiers of the newly empowered oligarchs, the King perused the ancient scroll and followed its instructions with meticulous care. Blood flowed freely through the streets of the city as a spell was cast in the palace. In the deepest hour of the night, the ritual was completed and the ivory statue stirred from its stillness. As the King stood entranced before it, stone turned to flesh, and his own flesh turned to fire. The newly born woman turned to her creator, looked in his eyes, and smiled.

When I try to imagine the unspeakable ecstasy he felt then, an experience of absolute bliss mingling with profound horror that threatened to destroy his sanity, it occurs to me that it was the idea of that single instant, that vision of the thing coming alive, that had been the source of his obsession all along. Perhaps it was neither his dissatisfaction with real women nor his desire for a sense of eternity that drove him to create and to love the statue. It was rather the experience of that moment when the boundary line between the animate and the inanimate, a living creature and an object, and life and death, is erased and he feels the terrifying joy of true freedom from all that binds him to the mundane world. He must have also felt godlike in his power to bring life where there was none, to witness his creation acknowledge that power, and to know that a sufficiently powerful imagination can overcome the strictures of what is called reality. The King let the flames of his exultation burn through his soul, annihilating the strength of his individual will, before he surrendered to the beckoning arms of his divine beloved.

In the first years of the despotic oligarchy, little was heard of the figurehead King living isolated in his dark palace. The servants and the caretakers of the place led quiet and fearful lives, hardly speaking of the strange lady who appeared out of nowhere to share the King's bed. Some accounts of his story end there, with the powerless King happy at last in his love, but others offer a more tragic ending to the tale.

The city states of the north were now at general war with one another, with constantly shifting alliances under a series of short-lived archons who fell in battle or at the hands of assassins. The colonies of the south revolted, and there were rumors that the grandson of the old emperor was preparing to lead his army out of the desert to reclaim his ancestral lands. In the ancient city, the governor declared himself king and slaughtered all those who opposed him, while the mad priest, who had become his chief advisor, prophesied the return of his mother the goddess. 'The firebird will come,' became the war cry of their soldiers as they fought the expeditionary force sent by the oligarchs to put down the revolt. The world burned and became drenched in blood while the King of the island enjoyed the favors of his lady in the dark. It was at this time that there were first sightings of enormous golden ships on the eastern horizon.

Some have written that the King fathered a daughter by his lover and that the chief port of the island was named for her. I am, however, skeptical of the idea for several reasons. First, even given the fantastic nature of the story, I find it implausible that a statue that was brought alive could give birth to new life in the normal manner. Second, it is unlikely that the King would have allowed such a birth to take place when he had avoided naturally born women all his life. Third, since there is no mention that the King destroyed the scroll of the forbidden art, there is no reason he could not have created another woman from a statue if that is what he desired. And fourth, I believe that the story of a daughter was a misinterpretation of the final apotheosis of the goddess.

One day, the servants of the palace saw a beautiful young girl at the bloom of her youth, who bore a striking resemblance to the King's lover, walk out of his chamber with light, graceful steps and a blissful smile shining on her face. As all who saw her gaped in amazement, she strolled out of the palace, through the streets of the city, and finally to the port in a kind of easy, willowy dance of joy. When she arrived at the end of a dock and faced the vast, undulating sea, she opened her arms in an invitation to an embrace. Witnesses say that she then transformed herself into a bird of fire and flew off into the great dome of the sky.

When servants came to bring the King his meal, they found him alone and were shocked to notice for the first time how old and emaciated he had become in only a few years. His eyes were empty and his breathing shallow as he lay on the soiled sheets of his bed. His lady was nowhere to be seen.

☯

"The firebird is coming," the mad priest told the soldiers of the ancient city that was now besieged by the army of the oligarchs. "I have seen the firebird fly in my dreams. It is coming. It is coming to save us and to bring us victory." But then the rebel king, the former governor, was struck down in the fighting by a javelin, the walls of the city were breached, and a great slaughter began. It was only when the door to the priest's chamber in the highest tower of the city was being smashed open that he looked out the window and understood that while the firebird indeed flew, it was not coming to the city. It was going elsewhere, to new lands.

"I have been abandoned by my mother," the priest calmly told the soldiers who broke in. "I must go to her. I must fly to her as she flies in the sky." Before they could stop him, he climbed onto the ledge of the window and stepped off into the air. He failed to turn into a firebird as he plunged down.

Only days after the city fell, it was attacked by a great southern army that came out of the desert with fierce, nomadic riders in their ranks. The northerners were taken by surprise and suffered great losses as they drew back to the coast to regroup. Their archons across the sea hurriedly sent reinforcements, and the two races began killing each other again.

After years of fighting, as the war was coming to a close due to sheer exhaustion and the depletion of soldiers on both sides, fleets of enormous golden ships arrived from the east and landed in key cities on both the southern and northern continents to unleash their countless gold-armored soldiers riding great, terrifying monsters and bearing awesome weapons of fire. In a matter of months, all the lands of both the old and the new races were subdued by this third race, a people who were known as the lords of the horizon.

There is no need for me to recount the history of the golden conquest for the elucidation of the story of the King and the statue, except to point out that the newcomers were believers in a single god who claimed that all other supernatural beings were either figments of the imagination or evil demons bent on leading humanity away from the path of the one god. Yet they did not try to impose their beliefs upon their subjects, allowing instead to let their power and glory demonstrate the fortunes of those who follow the true way. Just as the temples of the goddess in the ancient city had become empty after the conquest, people under the golden rule began to abandon their old deities in favor of the 'One who is the Only.'

In the ancient city, at the central temple of the goddess, the remaining priest, the simpleton, continued to take care of the place and to worship the image of the firebird. One day, he received a visit from an old man who claimed to be a faithful of the goddess as well. As the stranger seemed destitute and ailing, the priest allowed him to stay in a room at the back of the temple. Days passed, and as the priest went about his tasks, the old man helped where he could. They worshipped together, and shared modest meals in silence. The priest was used to solitude, but he found it nice to have a companion.

"When they write the story of the King and the statue," the old man suddenly spoke out as they sat in front of a mural of the firebird after their daily prayer, "they will write it as a story of men . . . of kings, priests, and sculptors. What they may neglect to show is that it was a woman, or rather a goddess, who was the central character, the one who was in control all along, the one who moved the others just as a game player moves the pieces on the board, the one who achieved her purpose in the end."

"What purpose?" the priest asked.

"I cannot know for certain. Not the whole of it, anyway. How can I? She was a goddess, and I . . . I am but a broken hearted old man who has lost everything but his memory. But I suppose I can surmise from what pieces of knowledge I have of her."

"She is beautiful," the priest said, staring at the image of the firebird.

"That she is. But she was much more than that. She was also cunning and cruel, but insects may say the same of us as we tread on them. We are insects beneath her luminous feet."

"She is a firebird."

"Yes. A firebird who wanted to fly once more. A firebird who no longer wanted to be a goddess bound to a city. The city is ancient, and she has been its patron deity for all that time, blessing it with fortunes, protecting it against its enemies, and loving its citizens as they loved her. But then she grew weary of the role she had played for centuries, she wanted to be free to roam the sky once more and to explore the wonders of the world. So she withdrew her favor from the city, and it fell to the barbarians. She then attached herself to the young prince of the conquerors, appearing in his dream and making love to him in it, to compel him to bring her into the world. She used a priest whom she had driven mad with visions of her motherhood, leading him to discover a forbidden scroll that contained the secrets of animation, and had him deliver it to the lover. He followed its instructions and incarnated her in a statue of his making.

"She was now in the world, but she needed to be infused with vital force to regain her full powers. This was achieved as her creator made love to her night and day, giving her the strength of life through his seed. Each time he spilled into her, he became weaker and she became stronger. Eventually, when he had no more life to give her, she left his palace, transformed herself into a firebird, and became free."

"How beautiful that must have been," the priest muttered.

"Yes. Beautiful. The most beautiful thing in the world."

Those were the last words of the old man as he slumped forward and died.

The last priest took his body and buried it in a yard at the back of the temple, shedding a few tears from his pure, innocent heart. A narrow shadow fell across the grave, from the lofty pillar upon which the King had first seen the vision of the goddess. On it now was a great golden globe. The lords of the horizon claimed that their one and only god was in the shape of a sphere, the center of which is everywhere and the circumference nowhere.

If one were to believe in the goddess and her escape as a firebird, one could follow the path of her long journey in legends, fairy tales, and historical records from all over the world. She is portrayed variably as a witch, a fairy godmother, a succubus, and a guardian angel. When she is not in a divine or magical form, she makes her appearances as a celebrated courtesan, a saintly nun, an intellectual noblewoman of a salon, a powerful empress, and a fierce revolutionary. Even in modern times, she is thought to have been a pioneering aviator, an influential anthropologist, an iconoclastic artist, a radical feminist leader, and a fashion model turned movie star. She is currently thought to be a renowned genetic biologist who also writes popular science fiction novels about female cyborgs.

> Then he ran home to see, to touch again
> The ivory image that his hands contrived,
> And kissed the sleeping lips, now soft, now warm,
> Then touched her breasts and cupped them in his hands;
> They were as though ivory had turned to wax
> And wax to life, yielding, yet quick with breath.
>
> —Ovid, *The Metamorphoses* (first century CE)

> "Statues, Asclepius, yes. See how little trust you have! I mean statues ensouled and conscious, filled with spirit and doing great deeds; statues that foreknow the future and predict it by lots, by prophesy, by dreams and by many other means; statues that make people ill and cure them, bringing them pain and pleasure as each deserves."
>
> —*Asclepius* (circa third century CE)

> And while [Donatello] was working on the [statue], he would stare at it, and kept saying to it: 'Speak, speak or be damned!'
>
> —Giorgio Vasari, *The Lives of the Artists* (1549—1550)

"If ever there was a model for this statue . . . and I doubt that Heaven ever brought forth such a woman, how I pity her lovers! She must have delighted in letting them die of despair. There is something ferocious in her expression, and yet I have never seen anything so beautiful."

—Prosper Mérimée, 'La Venus d'Ille' (1837)

The idea of the life of the statue is even more distinctly manifest in the so-called "pygmalionism," an imitation of this legend of Pygmalion and Galatea, and a utilization of this legend for erotic ends. Naked living women, in such cases, stand by as "statues" upon suitable pedestals, and are watched by the pygmalionist, whereupon they gradually come to life. The whole scene induces sexual enjoyment in the pygmalionist, who is generally an old, outworn debauchee.

—Iwan Bloch,
Das Sexualleben unserer Zeit in seinen Beziehungen zur modernen Kultur (1919)

. . . I would rather be a cyborg than a goddess.

—Donna Haraway, 'A Cyborg Manifesto' (1985)

HWANSANG OF MUNMYEONG

I. VENGEANCE

On the northernmost frontier of the vast empire that simply called itself the Central Nation, a single fur-clad warrior trudged out of the snowy hills, a great sword strapped to his back for beasts and bandits and a well-honed dagger in his belt meant for a single man. At the first town he reached in imperial territory proper, he entered the cheapest inn to rest for the night. The old proprietor, who had been a soldier until a war wound forced him to retire, considered his one and only patron as he served him a modest meal of stringy rabbit meat and boiled radishes. The warrior was too mature to be considered young, but his muscles were lean and taut, his face set in a determined frown, and his movements smooth and fast as a seasoned fighter's. Sensing that there was a story in the barbarian's journey, he offered the solid man a bottle of cheap wine gratis and inquired casually of his purpose in leaving the white hills.

"I seek a man who makes his home in Munmyeong," the warrior answered in a voice that was surprisingly boyish.

"Munmyeong, the great capital of the Central Nation?" the innkeeper asked.

"Yes."

"That is a long way to go, from the furthest of the periphery, to the center of the world."

"I have time and strength enough for it. I must, since finding him is the very purpose of my existence."

"And what purpose would that be?"

"Vengeance, a final reckoning. For I mean to kill that man, with this very blade," he said, indicating the dagger in his belt.

"A great crime he must have committed for a man to make his end the purpose of his life."

"That he did, upon my people and myself personally."

"Was he an imperial?"

"Yes. The commander of a great conquering army."

"You speak of the great northern expedition of two celestial cycles past?"

The warrior nodded. "He first came to our villages with just a few of his men, with a friendly mien and a box full of shiny treasures. He met with our chieftains, gave them gifts, and offered the embrace of the Empire. For our recognition of the Lords of Munmyeong as our masters, we would receive all the benefits of an outland province, including protection from our enemies, the introduction of imperial learning and crafts, and the inclusion of our gods into the family of the Lords of Heaven who favor the Central Nation above all nations in the world.

"Our chieftains discussed the offer among themselves, but decided that there was no reason to bargain away our freedom when we were strong enough on our own to fight our enemies, had no use for strange knowledge, and knew that the gods of our forefathers were the mightiest in Skyland. When they delivered their decision to the imperial commander, his visage turned dark, and he made threats of dire consequences if they did not reconsider. The chieftains were offended and threatened in turn to bind the strangers to trees for the wolves to feast on if they did not leave at once, and never show their faces in our land again.

"They left, but returned the following day with an army that swarmed over the land like a great storm cloud. Our chieftains and warriors fought bravely, but most fell from the first wave of imperial arrows that rained down upon them as they charged the enemy's endless shielded ranks. When all the men were dead or wounded, they moved onto our villages and began setting everything on fire, killing anyone, women, children, the old and the ailing, who stood in their way. In the course of a single day, our people, who had ruled the hills since All-Father set the first ancestors down upon the highest peaks a thousand years ago, were no more. Those few who survived the massacre were put in chains and sent off to unknown lands. There is nothing there now but an imperial fortress, manned by a frontier garrison."

The warrior stopped to take a large sip of the wine. The innkeeper allowed him a long moment to mull over the destruction of his people.

"And what is your story in that tragedy?" he finally asked.

"I was a son of a chieftain. My father was killed in the battle, and my mother and siblings all fell to imperial swords for resisting in our village. At the sight of my mother's detached head rolling on the ground, I gave into my fear and ran to the forest to hide with other cowards and weaklings. I was a mere child, but I also was the son of a chieftain. It was the most shameful moment of my life. But after darkness descended, when I could see the fires that were burning our villages, I remembered who I was and resolved to avenge my people. With this blade, given to me when I passed the test of the young warrior's agony," he indicated his dagger again, "I came out of the forest and headed for the home of my family.

"As luck, if it can be called that, would have it, I saw the imperial commander himself, standing by the flames of our house, exchanging some jovial words with his captains who laughed obsequiously at his jests. I approached him with stealth and pounced on him when the opportunity presented itself. My dagger should have entered his throat and choked off his evil breath for good, but he sensed my approach in the last moment. He took my wrist and twisted until the dagger fell out of my hand and I fell at his feet with the arm dislocated. Despite the pain and the humiliation, I yelled curses at him, which only amused him and his men.

"When I finally ran out of breath and could curse him no more, he chuckled and picked up my blade. In our tongue, which he spoke well, he told me how much he admired my courage for attempting to exact vengeance for my people instead of staying in the forest. Although I was filled with hatred, I was surprised at those words and looked up at his face. That was the first time I saw the scar across his left eye, which was discolored to a bluish hue, in sharp contrast to his dark right eye.

"'Ah, you notice my ruined eye,' he said in a friendly tone. 'That was the work of another such as you, a brave avenger. She was a priestess of another barbarian people, whose temple my men were sacking, but she was a bit more successful, as you can see. It is curious though that the wound turned out to be a blessing of sorts for me. I can see very little with it, a big disadvantage in a fight, but I get visions in it of sudden danger. Just now, when you came at me with your dagger, you should have been successful in dispatching me, but I had a distinct image of you jumping at me from the darkness a moment before you actually did. Thus I was able to disarm you. So many times have I avoided certain death thanks to such visions. I must have been cut by an enchanted blade, but then I killed the priestess in fury. That was a mistake, for I will never know the meaning of this blue eye and its power. Perhaps she meant for me to see something important through it, or she blinded me to that very thing.'

"He looked down with a suddenly melancholy expression as his captains looked about the burning houses all around us. After a long moment of contemplation, he took a step toward me.

"'I have a proposal for you, young avenger,' he told me. 'I will give you back your dagger and a fighting chance to survive. If you do, you will no doubt come seek me out. You can find me in Munmyeong, the great capital of the Central Nation, in the district of Junggu. If you make it there, you should have no trouble getting directions to the house of Hwansang of the Blue Eye, which is what I call myself. I will try to be ready for you, to be vigilant always for your coming, but you might get the best of me as I might be old and feeble-minded by the time you come. Use this dagger to kill me then, but before you do, you must swear to tell me of your adventures since this night, when I destroyed your people. Perhaps in your story I will learn something about myself that I lost when I killed that priestess. Swear to me that you will, and I will let you live.'

"It irked me to make a deal with him, and I thought of attacking him one last time, but I knew that would be a useless gesture. I wanted to live, not for myself since I had already given up on my life when I left my hiding place in the forest, but for the chance to avenge my people. So I agreed. I would come for him at his house in Munmyeong, in the district of Junggu, but I would tell him the stories of my adventure before I killed him."

"So here you are," the innkeeper said, "a warrior taking his first steps into the Central Nation, on the long journey to Munmyeong."

The warrior nodded and took another sip of the wine.

"And you no doubt have great stories to tell him."

"Too many. I hope the night is long enough when I finally get to him, for it will be under the cover of darkness that I will steal into his house. I will take him, for now I have the strength and the cunning to do so, but before I do, I will also tell him how I will seek out and kill all of his progeny, be they men, women, or children. He will go to his death knowing that I will end his blood line."

"So none of your hatred for him has abated through the years."

"It burns brighter than ever."

"But his progeny . . . perhaps they are innocent."

"As were mine, all of whom he murdered with one stroke of his blade."

"Surely you speak of your family, not your progeny, since you were a child when he came to you."

"I was. After that night, he sold me off as a slave. But he gave strict instructions to my master that I was to be trained as a fighter and that I was to be granted freedom in ten years, at which time my dagger must be returned to me. It was as hard a life as you can imagine, but I survived, grew strong, and when I became a free man, I worked as a mercenary, fighting in a hundred battles among the tribes of the valley."

"As terms of enslavement go, yours were generous," the innkeeper pointed out.

"Yes, but before he sent me away . . . " he stopped and looked down. He took another large sip of wine before continuing.

"Before he sent me away, he told me that our agreement was between the two of us only, that he looked forward to facing me in the future, but would not allow my progeny to carry on my blood feud against his if the two of us should fail to meet again. So he, somewhat apologetically, told me that he had to deprive me of all my offspring in advance. Before he returned my dagger, he used it, my own weapon, to cut out the source of my manhood."

The warrior hid his face in his hands and wept freely. When he recovered, the two of them finished the wine in silence as the wind howled outside.

Early next morning, as the warrior was about to resume his southward trek, the innkeeper came out to see him off.

"When you finally have Hwansang under the blade," the old man said, "will you tell him about me, of how you told your story to an old innkeeper on your first night in the Central Nation?"

"I will."

"Then tell him also that as you set out in the morning, he wished you luck upon your journey, and said that one such as he must meet such an end as he made for so many others, if not for justice, then for some semblance of reason in the world. Surely that is the lesson about himself that he must learn before he dies."

The warrior thought about those words, nodded to the innkeeper, and went on his way. The old man watched the solid sword-bearing form enter the morning fog and disappear into its frigid embrace, remembering the great northern expedition of two celestial cycles past when he, as a young soldier, first came to those parts, and participated in the destruction of all those who would not submit to the Central Nation, under the command of that great man they called the Conqueror of the North.

II. LOVE

At an oasis town on the western frontier of the Central Nation, a mature woman went out to the desert to await her husband's return from the nomad market. As the setting sun began to paint the sky in fiery shades, she saw him appear on the horizon, atop their great traveling beast. When they approached the town, she noticed that in addition to her husband and the burden of goods from the market, the beast also carried another figure, a slight bent form that bore something on its chest.

"I found them in the desert, on the verge of death," her husband told her as he slid off the beast and helped down the stranger, who turned out to be an emaciated young woman carrying a baby. "First the guests as the gods command," he said when his wife offered him a water skin, reminding her of their sacred duty to all visitors who may be envoys of the gods in disguise.

After a quick refreshment of water and fruit, they took the mother and child into town and to their modest dwelling, where the wife saw to the needs of the guests, while the husband, as per custom, went to stay the night at his father's house, so that the strangers might be more comfortable in his. The hostess provided them with water and helped them clean themselves, especially the baby boy who was sleeping soundly despite all the commotion. When they were finally made presentable with clean clothes, the wife examined the young woman and saw that she was very beautiful, despite the wear and tear of the desert, with large blue eyes, gracefully curving cheekbones, and full, yearning lips. She prepared dinner, cooking some precious beast meat in honor of the guests.

"You are not of the nomads," she asked the young woman as they shared the meal.

"No, kind hostess," she replied in a modest manner. "I am of a tribe of the Imperial Protectorate of the Three Wells."

"The Protectorate? You have journeyed far."

"And I must journey so much farther."

"Where do you mean to go?"

"To Munmyeong, the great capital of Central Nation."

"All the way there!" the woman exclaimed, as if she had said that she was going to the moon. "What business does a woman of the desert have there?"

The young woman bowed her head down and remained silent. Her hostess did not wish to be rude in questioning her further, so they finished the meal in silence. As she finished clearing away the plates, the baby began to cry. The young woman went to the boy and comforted him in her arms by trying to give milk, but found she was dry. The hostess brought some goat milk in a skin and offered it to the woman who took it with thanks. The baby calmed down as he began to drink and opened his eyes to the hostess, who was amazed that they were mismatched—one blue, like that of the desert people, and the other dark, like that of the imperials.

"So the father is an imperial," she said.

The young woman shed some tears, but soon regained her composure. The baby stared at them both as he drank heartily.

"Are you exiled from your people?" the hostess asked, wondering if she should let her be. But she had always been a curious person, constantly begging elders for stories as a little girl.

"No, but I would have been if I had stayed."

The hostess made a sympathetic sound before stroking the baby's soft hair, which made him smile brightly at her.

"Such a beautiful one," she said. "The gods have not graced our house with a child yet."

"May they do so in plenty and health," the young woman blessed, and the hostess nodded sideways in thanks.

"Do you seek the child's father in Munmyeong?"

"Yes."

"I hear it is a big town. Almost infinite, travelers say."

"He is Hwansang of Munmyeong, whose house is in the district of Junggu. He told me that once there I will have no trouble getting directions to it."

"He should have taken you, an imperial or not."

"He meant to, but he was taken away from me. We are bound, though, in body as well as spirit, so we are together in the dream world, where I see him every night. I just want him to see his son in this world, so that he may see the continuation of our love in him."

"How hard love is. A curse of demons."

"But a blessing of the gods as well. He was the greatest joy I have ever known."

"Was he a soldier, an administrator?"

"No, a servant. He served the daughter of the Imperial Viceroy at the City of Three Wells, where my father was a tribal councilman."

"A highborn woman you are, then," the hostess said in surprise. "Too high for a servant, imperial or not."

"He too is highborn," she asserted with some offence in her voice, though she immediately raised her palms to her in apology. "He is a scion of a noble family of Munmyeong, from the caste of the letter and the book, which is higher in the Central Nation than that of the spear and the warhorse."

"How was he a servant of a woman, then?"

"Because his uncle, the patriarch of his clan, committed a great wrongdoing for which he would have been executed, which would have meant that the entire family would have fallen from its status. Hwansang volunteered to a term of servitude to the family that suffered from the crime, since his uncle did not have a son to do so, which reduced the penalty to life imprisonment for the patriarch and allowed the family name to remain in the register of nobles. The clan to which he submitted himself had been a traditional enemy of his line, so they humiliated him by making him the bondman of a girl."

"Ah, the cruelty of the powerful. There in the capital of the Empire, as here."

The young woman nodded in agreement before continuing her story.

"The girl's father was appointed as the new Viceroy to the Protectorate almost as soon as he went into their service, so he accompanied the family here, to the furthest west of the Empire."

"It must have been a hard life for a wellborn like him."

"He said that it was in the beginning. The family abused him at every turn, and the girl made a plaything of him, teasing him and making him perform all manner of humiliating acts. But he bore it all, not only because he would have been dismissed for any act of disobedience, which would have led to his uncle's execution and his family's ruin, but also because he was genuinely ashamed of what the patriarch had done, and saw his servitude as a fitting price to pay for the removal of the stain on the clan's honor.

"During their long journey to the Protectorate, their convoy was raided by bandits in the middle of the night. In the skirmish, Hwansang did a great service to the family, fiercely protecting the Viceroy's daughter against a group of barbarians who meant to carry her off. He paid the price of a terrible wound, a cut across the left eye that made him nearly blind in it and discolored it to a bluish hue, like that of our eyes. After that incident, the family ceased to pick on him, allowing him some dignity in carrying out his tasks. The girl he served also stopped using him as the butt of pranks, as she secretly fell in love with him.

"They arrived at the City of Three Wells, and there we met. At the great banquet in which the tribal councilmen welcomed the new

Viceroy, my attention was drawn to the tall, handsome man with the blue and dark eyes, who looked so noble even as he served the young girl from the imperial capital. A few days later, I saw him at the market, going about on an errand, and I felt compelled to approach him, despite the fact that I had reached an age when I should act in a modest manner. We conversed, correcting each other as we only half knew each other's tongues, arranged to meet again, shared a meal to speak of ourselves, our worlds, our desires, and were in love like there was no one else in all the world.

"Once we confessed our love for each other, we thought of how we could be together always. A marriage between a desert person and an imperial was frowned upon by both sides at the Protectorate, but an official sanction was possible for the daughter of a councilman and a noble youth of the Empire, in the interest of strengthening the ties of the two races. He had to serve out his term of servitude, but once he returned to Munmyeong and reclaimed his status, he could then return to the City of Three Wells to apply for a marriage of alliance with me. It would take some years, but it was all quite possible."

"But he lay with you and abandoned you," the hostess said, regretting it as soon as the words left her mouth. She cursed her own impatience.

"No, he would never have done that to me. As I told you, we were bonded, physically and spiritually. We could not betray each other if we tried."

The two women saw that the baby had fallen asleep again, so the mother lay him down in the comfort of a blanket.

"During one of our meetings," she continued, "at the Garden of the West Well where he told me that his love for me was like a bottomless well, we were seen by a maiden of the girl he served. She told her mistress, who went mad with jealousy and sent another servant to spy on us. When she became certain of our affair, she summoned Hwansang and confessed her love for him before demanding that he become her lover. He tried to dissuade her, pointing out that such a relationship between them, if discovered, would result in immediate dismissal for him, but she remained adamant in her desire. The following day, she summoned him again, but she was told that he was nowhere to be found. When she had not seen him for another day, she finally lost her mind, tore at her own hair and clothes, and fell to the floor purposely to put bruises on her body. She then went out, screaming and weeping, just as her father was returning from an overnight mission to the desert to negotiate with the nomad masters. When the Viceroy asked what had happened to her, she claimed that Hwansang had come to her in the night and forced himself on her, to impregnate her with his child.

"'But that could not have been,' her father said, 'since Hwansang came with me, as he has become fluent in the tongue of the tribesmen and I needed one of us to spy on what they spoke of during our negotiations.' And Hwansang indeed came up to them from the Viceroy's train, puzzled at what was happening.

"The Viceroy took his hysterical daughter to his chamber and questioned her further on the matter. She confessed everything to him, including her love for Hwansang, which put her father in a quandary. The situation was an intolerable one, but the servant had done nothing wrong to deserve dismissal, he was exemplary even in his refusal to take advantage of the situation. In the end, the Viceroy decided to put Hwansang under the service of his aging aunt who lived with the family, and send them back to Munmyeong, so that he might serve out the rest of his term away from his daughter.

"On the night before his departure, Hwansang stole out of the Viceroy's mansion to meet me for the last time. We went out to the desert and made love for the first time under the light of the blessed moon. 'The first time,' he told me with tears streaming from his mismatched eyes, 'but not the last, I swear. When I am free again, I will come back for you. I will then take you back to Munmyeong, where we will live in our ancestral home in the district of Junggu. There we will raise our children, and be happy in our union.'

"And so he left," she said and shed some tears, as did the hostess.

"But then you became with child," the latter said in understanding.

"Yes. When my father learned of it, and I revealed the identity of my lover, he wept in shame and for my tragedy as well, as he treasured me beyond anything in the world. He kept me in isolation during my pregnancy, and told me that when I had the child, I would have to leave the Protectorate, lest I be cast out by the Council and thus carry the curse of the exile forever. The baby came, and it had one blue eye of our people, and one dark in the manner of the imperials, a sign of Hwansang's love. My father placed me with a reliable merchant whose caravan was heading east, but we were raided by bandits on the third day out and I barely escaped with my baby during the fight. That is how your kind husband found us in the desert."

"So you really mean to go all the way to Munmyeong, to find your lover."

"Yes, Hwansang of the Blue Eye, at the house in the district of Junggu."

As the young woman seemed exhausted, the hostess prepared a bed for her.

Next morning, she went to her husband and told him the gist of the guest's story. He felt pity for her also and made inquiries at the local market, until he found another caravan that was heading into the Central Nation. As its master was a friend, he agreed to take the mother and child on and guarantee their safety.

The guest said many thanks to her hosts before she left with her child. The hostess was watching the line of traveling beasts start on the great road east, feeling sad in her heart for the young woman, when she suddenly remembered an imperial train that had passed through the town many months ago. She was amazed that she had not recalled it before, but she could distinctly picture a tall, handsome man who rode with the group, his head bowed down as he wept bitterly, his tears hiding the mismatched colors of his eyes.

III. SALVATION

The priest of a small, decrepit temple of the Lords of Heaven at the southernmost frontier of the Central Nation, was awakened in the middle of the rainy night by banging on the door of his domicile that frightened him. As he had few duties beyond conducting monthly blessings for the garrison of imperial legionnaires at the nearby fortress, the only time he was paid an unexpected visit was to be notified of an imminent raid by the savages of the jungle. He would have to quickly gather what essential things he could and run to the safety of the fortress before dark shadows emerged from the trees with javelins and clubs.

When he hurried to the door and opened it, he was astonished to see a single savage standing in the rain, dressed in the saffron cloak of priesthood, the wooden beads of the celestial cycle around his neck.

"Oh, Holy Diviner of the Heavenly Way," the savage spoke in passable imperial tongue, "I beg shelter from the rain and the dangers of the night, from one Diviner to another."

"You, a priest?" he asked incredulously.

"Yes, Holy Diviner, though a mere jungle dweller I may be. I have been instructed on the ways of the nine virtues and the nine vices, I have learned the true tales of the cycles of the Lords of Heaven, and I have gone through the Purification Rite of Self Eradication. I am my own no longer, but an instrument of the Lords of Heaven."

The priest stared at the skinny brown man for a long time, not knowing what to make of this savage who knew the formulas of the Heavenly Way so perfectly, when all of his own attempts to convert the natives had led to utter failure, often ending in an eruption of violence necessitating the intervention of the legionnaires' spears. The savage was shivering, and looked badly in need of nourishment and rest, so the priest decided to trust in the signs of the Way and motioned for him to enter.

"Thank you, Holy Diviner, thank you," the savage said as he stumbled in. "May the Lords of Heaven grant you much ease and fortune. I do not think I could have lived another day out there."

"You are coming in from the jungle?" the priest asked.

"Yes, Holy Diviner."

"With no weapon and no gear?"

"I lost it all, along with all of my fellow pilgrims, to the unholy violence of the savages."

The priest was surprised to hear him refer to his own people in that manner. He led him into his sitting chamber where he bade him rest before bringing some water and food for him. The savage ate and drank ravenously, pausing only to thank him profusely for his kindness and wishing more blessings upon him.

"So you are a pilgrim," the priest asked when the dark man was refreshed.

"Yes, Holy Diviner."

"What is your destination?"

"Munmyeong, the great capital of the Central Nation, Holy Diviner. But it is not a place I seek, but a person."

"And who might that be?"

"A Holy Diviner like yourself, he who is called Hwansang of the Blue Eye."

"And what has this Hwansang done that he merits such a long and dangerous pilgrimage?"

"He saved us, Holy Diviner, all of my people. From our savage ways and the certain doom of eternal darkness. When he first came to us, we were no different from those animals who murdered my friends. He showed us the Heavenly Way."

"A priest went to your people through the jungle? How is it that I have not known of this?"

"We believe that it was the Lords of Heaven who brought him to us, Holy Diviner. They took pity on our lowliness and granted us the blessing of his coming."

"But the Lords of Heaven do not drop someone from the sky. They fashioned us with legs so that we may travel on our own."

The priest was surprised again to see the savage touch his ears to ward off the effect of evil words as if he had said something blasphemous. He was about to berate him for it, but then thought that if this dark priest regarded this Hwansang as such a holy person, even a harmless jest would be unseemly.

"So how did he appear to you?" the priest asked, his curiosity now aroused.

"Out of nowhere, Holy Diviner. Our men were returning from the hunt when they saw him standing at the edge of our village. A tall man, mature but not yet old. He wore the robe of the Diviner and the beads of the celestial cycle, though we did not know what they were at the time. Our spearmen, who were savages then, would have struck him down for the intrusion into our land, had they not been frightened by his eyes, one normal, the other blue, like that of a demon, and marked by a scar. He stared at us with those uncanny eyes until we all had to step back and look away from their power."

"What did he do then?"

"After he subdued our men with his glare, he stalked into our village and stood before the central fire mound. We all feared him and hid in our huts, but we could not help stealing glimpses at him through the doors. He stood there in perfect stillness for a long time, until he suddenly began to speak in our own tongue. He told us that we were all hopeless savages who led low lives, destined for a dark place full of ghostly beasts after our deaths. All of our gods were mere demons who fool simple people into worshipping them as gods and who delight in the misery and anguish of their subjects. Our shamans were their tools, and their powers were mere tricks of a charlatan. But he, Hwansang of Munmyeong, had come to us to save us, to teach us the Heavenly Way and help us live like a civilized people. He would not only teach us truth, but also make us prosperous and strong, to live in plenty and to defeat the onslaught of our enemies. We must accept his teachings and change our ways, or else we will be cast in darkness forever.

"When he fell silent again, our shamans became angry at his words and began to speak against him, saying that he was a demon who came to confound us. They gathered enough courage to charge the stranger, knock him down to the ground, and bind him with rope. When we saw how easily the shamans subdued him, we came out of our huts and gathered around the prone man.

"One of the shaman was about to kill him with a club, when Hwansang looked into his eyes, which made him avert his and turn away. He then got up again and looked at all of us, forcing us to turn away, before proclaiming that if we did not heed his words, the sun would go out the following day and never return."

'The eclipse,' the priest immediately thought, remembering the event of a celestial cycle past. 'Like the Imperial Stargazers, this Hwansang somehow knew about the coming of the eclipse, when the Lord of the Sun hides his face in his hands in sorrow at the sufferings of mankind. He used it to beguile these savages.' A part of him knew that if he had been privy to such information from the Stargazers, he would surely have used it also to convert the natives.

"The shamans wanted to kill him," the savage went on, "but our chief held them back, fearful that the stranger may be speaking the truth. He ordered him to be put into the hut of the unclean. Next day, the sun indeed went out, and we knew that it was all as he had said. The shamans ran from our village screaming in terror, never to be seen again, so we released the stranger and went down on our knees to beg him to return the light of the sun to us. He made us swear to follow his instructions in accepting the Heavenly Way, and to change our habits to become a civilized people. Then he brought the day back to us.

"In the next years, he not only taught us the nine virtues and the nine vices, and the true tales of the cycle of the Lords of Heaven, he delivered us from our savagery. Although we continued to hunt and gather, he ordered us to clear the land and plant seeds so that we may take food from the earth, and to bring certain animals into our village and raise them as docile beasts. He also taught us how to make better weapons and adopt cunning tactics in fighting our enemies; he had us build sturdy walls of logs to keep them off our land and houses that were raised above the ground to keep the floor dry even during the rainy season. He told us that the mutilation of our women's genitals was an abomination and that they were not to be treated as properties of men, but as equal members of the tribe. Our knowledge of the clean and unclean was all nonsense based on superstition, he instructed, and gave us a new classification of what was good for the health of our bodies and what was not. We were commanded to wash ourselves as thoroughly and as often as possible, to clean our clothes and dwellings constantly as the Lords of Heaven looked unkindly on dirty places and caused miniscule demons to descend upon them to wreak havoc on the inhabitants. We all had to learn the Imperial Script and the Imperial Numeric, and were encouraged to use them at every opportunity, to keep track of our properties, to write down our transactions, and to record our tales and those of our forefathers so that those after us would know of them. He chose those of us who exemplified a special talent for learning, including myself, and taught us the Imperial tongue. In that wondrous language, he told us of the marvels of the Central Nation, its great capital Munmyeong that is almost endless, and of all its great provinces from the snowy lands of the north and the sandy protectorates of the west to the hundred islands of the Eastern Ocean. We were amazed to hear that our world, our jungle, which we always thought to be the only one beneath Heaven, was but a small backwater on the southernmost edge of the Empire, and our people but the most savage race.

"After several years under his care, we came to know plenty and security as we never had before. We had ample food from the earth and from husbandry, few died from disease, and our enemies were repelled with ease. When some of the neighboring tribes became united by their jealousy of our success and sought to attack us in unison, Hwansang organized a preemptive attack on them using Imperial war strategy. Our warriors defeated them in a matter of days with few casualties on our side. Before they could go into a victory frenzy, however, he commanded us not to slay the captured warriors nor treat their people as slaves, but to show mercy, to persuade them with gentle words to adopt our ways and become one with our people. For that, we seemed like gods to them, as they had expected nothing but death at our hands. In no time, we were the ones who were teaching them how to farm the land, raise the beasts, to use letters and numbers, to be clean, and to follow the Heavenly Way. We became masters of nine tribes who all lived in peace and prosperity."

"How many days' journey into the jungle is your village?" the priest asked, fascinated by his tale.

"Many days, Holy Diviner, many days. Over a great hill, and across three rivers. We lost count while we were being chased by savages."

"So, now you seek Hwansang at Munmyeong. How did he come to leave you?"

The savage looked down in sadness for a moment before speaking again.

"That is a tragic tale, Holy Diviner, one that brings pain to my heart to recount.

"There was a little girl among us whom Hwansang took care of. Her father was one of the few who were killed during the war against the tribes, and her mother died during childbirth while we were away. Hwansang adopted her and adored her as his own. Several years later, after peace was well established in our land, the girl grew sick and could not stand anymore. Hwansang nursed her day and night, used all of his knowledge to try to bring her health back. But after many days of the effort, the girl died. The event not only caused much sorrow, it also brought a tremendous doubt upon him. He withdrew into his house, never opening his doors, except to accept a single meal every other day. We grew worried about him, and our leaders went to him to inquire after his well being, but he did not respond.

"After months of such isolation, he suddenly appeared at his door and asked for several of us younger men whom he had picked to learn the Imperial tongue. We, seven in number, sat with him in his house and he told us the tale of how he became who he is.

"Once, he was a nobleman from one of the most illustrious families of Munmyeong, who lived in the ancestral home in the district of Junggu. When his wife gave birth to a daughter, he loved that child with his entire being. But the girl fell ill, and he did everything in his power to cure her, summoning the most famed healers of the capital. The child died, however, and he fell into a great despair, feeling that there was no sense and reason to the world. To deliver him from his endless mourning, his wife brought a Holy Diviner of the Heavenly Way who counseled him on his grief. Accepting the doctrines of the Heavenly Way, he took up the meditative method, and looked deep within for some answer the Lords of Heaven might have for him. After months of solitary contemplation, he received a powerful vision in which he was visited by a Lord of Heaven who told him that he was deprived of his daughter because he was a vain and useless man who did not deserve the blessing such a child. When Hwansang asked how he could redeemed himself, he was told that he must make a sacrifice to see into the essence of things and use what he learns to do good in the world.

"When he came out of the meditation, he knew exactly what he had to do. He took a knife and cut himself across the left eye, which left him nearly blind in it, but allowed him to indeed see the essence of things and made him wise in all matters. He then left his ancestral home in the district of Junggu and entered a temple of the Heavenly Way to become a Holy Diviner. After he took the Purification Rite of Self Eradication, he left Mounmyun and became a wandering priest until he came to our land. He told us that when he saw the little girl he had adopted, he thought that it was his daughter reborn, that it was a gift of the Lords of Heaven for having delivered us from savagery. But she was taken away from him again, and he did not know why.

"'So it is apparent that my journey of redemption is not over,' he told us. 'And I have been meditating on how I may complete it. The Lords of Heaven have not revealed the answer to me, but they did tell me that it must be done in my old home, in Munmyeong. So I must leave you all and return to that place.'

"We wept in sorrow and fear that he would depart from us, but he assured us that we were now capable of living as civilized people without him. He also wanted to leave us with Holy Diviners of our own, so he performed the Purification Rite of Self Eradication for the seven of us, and made us priests of the Heavenly Way."

"And so he left you," the priest said in understanding, "yet now you seek him again."

"Yes, Holy Diviner. He told us that he would make a blessing upon us in prayer every day, but if a great calamity we are powerless against should befall us, we should seek him out in Munmyeong, in the district of Junggu, where we are to ask directions to the house of Hwansang of the Blue Eye."

"Your people are in danger then."

"Diseases none of has ever seen before are killing our children. Our crops have failed to grow, and we are reduced to hunting and gathering again. Renegade tribes of savages who refused to accept our ways are making constant attacks on us. We have been faithful to the Heavenly Way, but we are on the path to annihilation, and we do not know why. All seven of us who were made Holy Diviners left on this pilgrimage many days ago, but I am the only one who made it out of the jungle. I am the only remaining hope for our people."

As the hour was now very late, the priest suggested that they call it a night and gave him the only bed to rest on. Next morning, he took the trouble to accompany him to the fortress so that he would not be harassed by the soldiers. He met with the garrison commander and vouched for the dark man's status as a true Diviner of the Heavenly Way and asked for his help in getting him safe passage into the Central Nation. The commander was skeptical at first, being used to facing savages only with the spear, but he was finally persuaded to write up an Imperial order of protection for the dark priest and allow him to accompany the supply train that was returning to the interior.

As the priest saw him off, he suddenly remembered how more than a full celestial cycle ago, a soldier had come to the temple to deliver a message that a wandering madman with a scar across an eye who had been picked up by a patrol, had escaped from the stockade and was wandering about the area. They had never caught up with him again, but a few days after the priest had been notified, he had found a priestly robe and a set of wooden beads of the celestial cycle to be missing from the temple.

IV. JUSTICE

"Justice, I believe," the island magistrate told the Captain of an Imperial merchant ship as they ate dinner in his cabin, "is not an outcome, or an effect, of civilization, but its essence. A society without rational laws can never be a true civilization, whereas a community where justice prevails is a civilized place, whether it has what most would consider to be the trappings of civilization or not. Now how one . . . "

"So what you are saying," the Captain interrupted, "is that even if you have a group of people who walk about naked, live in caves, and eat human flesh, as long as they have good laws among them, they should be considered civilized."

"Not they, their society."

"What is the difference?"

"If, despite the lowliness of their ways, they indeed have come up with an arrangement that guarantees justice for all of their number, then that is something we should learn about, without, uhm, the nudity and cannibalism. Take the opposite case as well, the island state of Sunrise, the richest source of gold, silver and precious gems known to man. The inhabitants believe the place to have been the home of a treasure-hoarding god who grew sick of it all one day and departed, leaving it all to their forefathers. With the wealth they possess, it could have become a place of universal prosperity. Yet its oligarchs possess it all, and oppress the people in the most vicious manner for fear that they might rise up and take the riches away. You have been to its port, have you not?"

"Many times. Its magnificence is second only to that of Munmyeong."

"Yes, but you must have also noticed how miserable its common people are amidst all that splendor. How they live in anxiety and silence, lest the oligarchs' agents decide to make examples of them. There is no justice there, so it is not a civilized place."

"I still don't see your point," the Captain said with a shrug while dispatching the last of his fried fish.

"Let me ask you this then, Captain," the magistrate said. "You know our island well. What is your impression of it?"

The Captain thought about it. "It is as decent a place as any. Not much trading, but no trouble either."

"Ah, you are being diplomatic Captain," he said with a laugh. "You have explored the splendors of the hundred islands of the Eastern Ocean. It would not offend me to know that you found ours a rather shabby place, with no great sight to behold and no resources to be exploited. The only reason imperial ships come is that it's a convenient place to stock up on supplies before and after the long journey to the Pristine Morning Archipelago."

The Captain shrugged in general agreement.

"Our people freely admit to the lackluster nature of our home, because we have put our pride elsewhere, in our system of justice which we consider to be the best in the world. While the people of Sunrise believe that their ancestors were the caretakers of their god's treasures, we believe ours to have been the students of a philosopher-sage who concerned himself most of all with the nature of justice."

"Wait, I did have an experience of this system of justice you are so proud of," the Captain said, remembering. "Once we lost bags of sugar to the sea because the boat that was delivering them to our ship capsized. Since we had already paid for them, I thought that it was our loss."

"Ah, but one of our magistrates investigated without even being asked to."

"That's right. When they found out that the boat was in disrepair before it took on the cargo, they made the boatman pay us a third of the cost, and the merchant a third for hiring him without checking his boat."

"And you incurred the rest of the loss because you too could have sent a man to check the reliability of the deliverer. Let me ask you this, Captain, how did that experience make you feel?"

"Uhm. . . . it was refreshing, I suppose. Every island I go to, the merchants and magistrates are always trying to cheat us. I have to abide by imperial rules so as not to cause problems for our trade network, but I cannot count the times I have had to use the threat of our swords to discourage dishonest dealings by the locals. It was rather pleasant knowing that I would not have to worry about that on your island."

"Excellent. Now, Captain, if you had to make the choice between spending the rest of your life as an ordinary citizen of Sunrise or as one of our island, which would you choose?"

"An ordinary citizen? Why yours, of course."

"You are a civilized man, a citizen of the Central Nation. Sunrise is more like the Empire in its wealth, but our island is more like it in its laws. You chose ours, which means that despite the shabbiness of our home, it is more civilized than Sunrise."

The Captain thought about the magistrate's reasoning for a while, giving the latter a chance to finish his fish.

"I see what you are saying," the Captain said, "but then I must ask what you are doing on my ship. You told me that you mean to go to Munmyeong, which is a very long away. Why would you leave your home of perfect justice to travel to the mainland?"

"For the sake of justice, of course."

"Is it to be found in Munmyeong?"

"Not it, but a man, who must be held accountable for an injustice."

"What has he done that your island is sending a magistrate all the way over there?"

"As crimes go, it was not that serious. He cheated some of our people out of modest sums. But the size of the crime has never mattered to us. If even the most minor injustice is allowed to prevail, it invalidates the entire system."

"But surely, to go across the Empire . . . "

"That is precisely what the criminal counted on, Captain. That we would be dissuaded by distance and the hardship of travel from demanding satisfaction from him. He even told us where we could find him. In the district of Junggu, at the house of Hwansang of the Blue Eye."

"And what exactly did this Hwansang do to your people?"

"He came to us as a maritime official of the Central Nation. He wore the garb and bore the seals, so there was no reason for any of us to doubt him. His visage was rather uncanny since he had a scar across his left eye which was discolored to a bluish hue. He was given an official welcome by our leaders, with a banquet and entertainment, and he appeared dignified and gracious through it all, but would not reveal his purpose on our island, except that it was imperial business of great importance. In the next few days he could be seen around the ports, taking measurements, making notes, and asking fishermen and officials about the waters in the area. One night, he apparently got a bit drunk at the inn he was staying in and confided to its owner that the Empire planned to send a major expedition to the Pristine Morning Archipelago, to subdue its sealords and build a permanent base there. Our island would be the springboard for the mission, but a bigger port was required to harbor the fleet. The plan was to transport large boulders and much earth to the southern end of the great bay and use them to connect the land to the islet of Seapoint, thus enclosing the space for a port facility. It was fantastic, the very idea of raising land out of the sea, but we had seen those enormous golden ships that sailed out to the Eastern Ocean, vessels the size of islands that could very well bring enough material for the purpose."

"As has been done before," the Captain claimed. "In the bays across the eastern coast, new lands were created by cutting down entire hills and moving them into the sea."

"The wonders of the Central Nation."

"Yes, but a fictitious one in your case, since I would have heard something about it if it had been true."

"Indeed. Our people are not a particularly gullible lot, but it was a rather fabulous story this Hwansang told. I have found that receptivity toward a lie decreases as its claims become grander, but that when it reaches a certain level of magnitude, it suddenly gains power to convince by the sheer power of it extravagance."

"You mean a big lie is more easily believed than a little one?"

"A big lie invites skepticism, but an enormous lie invites faith."

"Ah."

"A new land connecting the islet to the island, who would have thought of it? Anyway, word got around about the secret plan, and it made a lot of people very excited. Some approached Hwansang for more details, but he refused to speak of the matter. Many took that as a kind of confirmation of the innkeeper's tale.

"After several weeks, the visitor became quite intimate with some of our citizens, mostly those who socialized at the inn he was staying at. Eventually, he took some of them into his confidence, swore them to silence, and told them they could purchase, in advance, pieces of the new land that would be created, for a very modest price."

"I see."

"Although it would take some years, having a shop or an eatery there could be a great boon when the imperial fleet would be docked in the new port. Hwansang claimed that he had the necessary paperwork to guarantee people a spot on the land when the work was completed. Each person who bought into the lie thought that he was the only one on the island who was given this opportunity, and each of them, remarkably enough, kept his mouth shut since Hwansang told them that it could ruin the whole project if others learned of it."

"How many people did he swindle?"

"Quite a few, securing only a modest sum from each, but added up, he made a killing. When some of them hesitated about handing him the money, he swore by saying, may his other eye be cut if he is lying. He then told a story of how he had once made a business deal which had gone awry and had put him in a situation where he could not fulfill his part of the bargain. As he had not been to blame for the situation, his contractor had agreed to forgive him, but he had been overcome by remorse at not having taken better care of his business, and had cut himself across the eye. That, he claimed, would be a perennial reminder to be upright and careful in all of his dealings."

The Captain chuckled at that. "Someone who discovered one of his frauds probably did that to teach him a lesson."

The magistrate nodded in agreement. "Then he disappeared one day, taking an imperial ship back to the mainland. He left a note at the inn that said that he had received a letter informing him that the expedition to the Archipelago had been cancelled, that there would be no construction of new land on our island. He apologized for not having returned the money, but claimed that he was in a hurry to catch the ship. He concluded by saying that anyone who wished to reclaim their money could do so in Munmyeong, the great capital of the Central Nation, in the district of Junggu, at the house of Hwansang of the Blue Eye.

"It was a taunt, really. He did not expect anyone to come all the way across the sea and the Empire for the modest sum he lost."

"But he did not count on the way of your people. Justice, no matter how small."

"Yes."

"What a hardship on you, though. Away from home on such a long journey. Where is the justice in that?"

"Oh, I will be rewarded enough when I return. And it will erase my shame as well."

"Shame, from what?"

"From having been one of those whom Hwansang swindled, one of those who believed his story of the new land, and of his cut eye. The only magistrate and educated person to have fallen for his lie. Believe me, Captain, it was a great relief to leave the island, to escape my colleagues' sneers and taunts."

The Captain nodded with a smile, finally understanding. "So you will undertake this journey, find this Hwansang at the district of Junggu, march into his house and demand your money and that of the other victims."

"Oh, I will do more than that," the magistrate said.

"What will you do?"

Suddenly, the magistrate whipped out a large curved blade from his jacket, that shook in fury.

"With this blade I will cut that brigand's other eye!" he yelled, his face flushed with anger, making the Captain lean back with fright. "That was part of the deal! May his other eye be cut if he is lying! And he lied to me! The bastard lied to me! I will have my money back, and my dignity as well, but I will also have his eye! For that is justice! That is justice! Do you understand? Justice!"

A week later, when the ship finally docked at a port of the imperial mainland, the Captain saw the island magistrate disembark his ship. Although he had avoided him since that dinner, his story had never left his mind, something about it nagging at his memory. As he watched the magistrate disappear into the crowd at the port, he suddenly remembered the time he had bought barrels of fruit from a merchant with a blue eye who sold them at a bargain price. Once they were out to sea, his men had discovered that below the top layer of fruit, the barrels were filled with rocks.

IV. HWANSANG AT MUNMYEONG

After many months of traveling filled with danger and hardship, a lone warrior from the northern hills, a mother and her child from the western desert, a dark priest from the southern jungle, and a magistrate from the Eastern Ocean arrived on the road to the great gates of Munmyeong where all imperial roads converged. As they approached the city, however, they witnessed things that made them wary—raggedy groups of imperial troops marching out, looking exhausted and demoralized; groups of barbarians on horseback riding to and fro, some letting out war cries; and great pillars of smoke from nearby settlements. When they came to the edge of the Munmyeong, they found its great gates smashed to pieces and the entire city in ruin.

It was only then that they realized that the Central Nation had fallen, that while they journeyed from the far edges of its empire, barbarians had defeated its great army, besieged its capital, and sacked it when it fell to them. They had only recently departed, leaving nothing but the smoldering skeleton of the city filled with the countless corpses of its citizens. Somehow the warrior, the mother and child, the priest, and the magistrate came together as they made their way through the destruction of Munmyeong. They asked directions of the dazed and destitute survivors to the district of Junggu, which they found to be atop the highest hill of the city. They climbed it in silence, too stupefied by the devastation around them to even inquire after one another's identity and purpose in seeking Hwansang.

Once they were on the hill, they asked another traumatized survivor for the house of Hwansang of the Blue Eye. He wordlessly pointed at a nearby ruin of a mansion, all burnt and smashed. The travelers entered the property and wandered about the remains of the house they had dreamt of for so many nights. They looked around, hoping to find something, some sign of what they must do now. All things of value had been taken by the barbarians and the rest destroyed beyond recognition, offering no clue to the enigma of their former owner. The bodies they found were of servants, some of them violated in the most heinous manner.

Hours passed and the sun began to set, turning the sky blood red as if polluted by the great carnage below. The travelers gathered at the destroyed front gate as if they had agreed to do so and walked out together. A short distance away, they discovered a fallen statue of bronze, lying across a grave with a stone marked with the characters of the ancient imperial ideograph, rather than the modern phonetic script, which none of the travelers could read. The statue, however, they all recognized as that of the one they had journeyed so far to meet, the eye-scarred man in a nondescript robe, looking down perhaps in contempt at those below him, or in sadness at his fate, or in contemplation of his condition, or in shame of his deeds.

When the travelers grasped that Hwansang of the Blue Eye lay in the grave before them, one of them wept to be deprived of purpose in life, feeling lost in a world without meaning; another experienced a sense of liberation from a great burden and realized that all things were possible in the future; another went mad with grief and anger, beginning on a path of destruction that would end only in death; and the last realized that it was not Hwansung of Munmyeong each of them had sought, that he was only a beacon in the quest to understand the mystery of their own lives, a sign long since revealed to them in the course of their long journey to the non-existent center of the world.

THE BEAUTIFUL AND USEFUL MACHINE: AN INTELLECTUAL HISTORY

In the heart of the country was the City of the Machine, and in the heart of the city was the beautiful and useful machine. During the heyday of the nation, one could find in its libraries, universities and temples, literally hundreds of stories on the nature of the machine, with a great variety of ideas on its origin, the identity of its creator, and the truth of its purpose. When the country entered the modern age, however, its historians took care to research every single one of those tales and found not a shred of real evidence that supported any of them. It should be of no surprise that the scholars should have spent so much effort on the project, since the entire intellectual history of the culture was based on myriad competing ideas about the great enigma of the machine. But as the leading figure of the philosophical movement of Mechano-skepticism pointed out, there were only three facts about the machine that anyone could be certain of.

First, the machine was inscrutable, as its uniform surface was seamless and apparently indestructible and featured no markings of any kind. Second, the machine was useful, as it not only provided all kinds of services for the entire country, but it also periodically revealed new practical functions. And third, the machine was beautiful, in its singular shape, both simple and perfect, and in the perpetual sound of its mechanical workings which was like the music of luminous rain on a melancholy autumn morning. In fact, the machine was the most inscrutable, useful, and beautiful thing anyone had ever seen in the world.

☯

In that elusive and magical moment when the people of the nation emerged from the darkness of prehistory by recording their myths, memories, and activities, they began by relating how their nomadic ancestors came upon the machine in the middle of an uninhabited land and settled around it to gaze at its beauty and listen to its mesmerizing song. They soon discovered wondrous uses for the machine and praised it for its benevolence. With time, the praise turned to worship, and worship, in turn, gave rise to a religion with all the trappings of rituals, symbols, and a hierarchy of priests. The first theologian asserted that since the machine is good to the people, it is a good thing, and therefore the Creator of the machine must be good. From that simple reasoning, an entire system of sacred metaphysics and ethics was created, its central ideas becoming the orthodox tenants of the Church of the Machine, which in turn provided the foundation for social order and political authority.

The establishment of the Church inevitably gave rise to heresy, the most radical form of which questioned the goodness of the machine and therefore the goodness of its Creator. "The usefulness of the machine is not a good, but a temptation," the first heresiarch claimed. "See how it offers us new temptations at every turn. The more useful we find the machine, the more helpless we become. It seeks to enslave us by making us dependent upon it. Slavery is an evil, therefore the machine is evil. The machine is evil, therefore its Creator is evil. For the Evil Creator's plan to be thwarted, the machine must be rejected." He also told stories of the distant past when their wandering ancestors were free and innocent, until they came upon the machine and unwittingly bound themselves to its diabolical power. Those discontent with the status quo of the society flocked to the movement, which came to be called 'Mechano-rejectionism,' and the nation experienced its first religious strife, persecution, and, eventually, civil war.

For a brief time in the conflict, the Mechano-rejectionist force gained control of the City of the Machine. During that period, its leaders not only forbade the use of the machine but also attempted to destroy it by every means available to them. They discovered, however, that they could neither make a single dent on it nor move it from the place where their ancestors had first found it. They then began to bury it under large rocks, but the citizens of the city, whose life had become very difficult without the benefit of the machine's useful works, arose in general revolt and ousted the Mechano-rejectionists from the place.

After years of fruitless and bloody fighting, a pragmatic ruler of the City of Machines sought to bring the war to an end by offering the heretics an edict of religious tolerance if they would put down their arms and swear to leave the machine alone. Exhausted and demoralized by the hardships of the long conflict, most of the Mechano-rejectionists agreed, and the fanatic few who carried on the fight were quickly eradicated. Historians have pointed to a number of reasons for the subsequent decline of Mechano-rejectionism in peacetime, including the failure of its quarrelsome leaders to form a single organized religion as an alternative to the Church of the Machine, limitations to social advancement for those who openly avowed the belief, and intellectual trends that, in reaction to the costly war, rejected religious fanaticism in general and sought knowledge on a more rational basis. There is a general agreement among scholars, however, that the most important cause of the eclipse of the heresy was the continuous and expanding usefulness of the machine with no apparently negative side effect. In a sense, the first heresiarch was right in predicting that the civilization would become increasingly dependent upon the machine. Yet no diabolical design of the Evil Creator nor a cataclysmic future of an enslaved humanity could be discerned in it. As its beneficial works were accepted by most people as a natural part of everyday life, the final remnant of diehard Mechano-rejectionists left the City of the Machine and then the land altogether, in order to escape its presence.

☯

At a recent academic conference I attended on the history of the country, a young scholar presented a fascinating revisionist paper on the fate of Mechano-rejectionism in the post-war period. His bold thesis was that the belief, far from dying out, was transformed by a new generation of intellectuals into the philosophical movement of 'Mechano-finitism.' "Mechano-rejectionism lost the war on the battlefield, but it triumphed as Mechano-finitism in the halls of universities," he asserted, causing much excitement as well as indignation among his colleagues.

The central idea of Mechano-finitism is simple. Everything in the world that is finite in size is finite in duration also. The machine is in the world and finite in size, therefore it must be finite in duration as well. In other words, as useful and dependable as the machine is, it must come to a stop at some point in the future. The danger then of blindly relying upon it is not that it will enslave us to some evil being, but that it will leave us utterly helpless when it ceases to work.

In order to support the idea that this is a secular version of Mechano-rejectionism, the historian made three points. First, most of the proponents of the movement were from Mechano-rejectionist clans, its most prominent thinker being the direct descendant of a major heresiarch during the war. Second, there were numerous ideas in their works that were taken right out of Mechano-rejectionist writings, including terminology and metaphors idiosyncratic to the belief. And third, the Church of the Machine quickly condemned the movement on the grounds that it smacked of Mechano-rejectionism.

In the lively discussion that ensued, one senior historian objected that while it is reasonable to speak of the influence of Mechano-rejectionism on Mechano-finitist philosophy, it would be wrong to identify them so closely, since the latter is utterly devoid of the millenarian spiritualism that is at the heart of the former. Another scholar criticized the notion of the triumph of Mechano-rejectionism in the rise of Mechano-finitism,over the Church of the Machine. He pointed out that it was not really Mechano-finitism itself that won out but Neo-mechano-finitism which appeared two generations later, a philosophy that was formulated by scholars for whom the conflict between the heresy and Church orthodoxy was no longer an issue. Yet another historian showed that by the time Mechano-finitism appeared, 'Mechano-rejectionism' was a catchall label the priests attached to any view which deviated from that of the Church, and so the condemnation cannot count as evidence of a link between the heresy and the philosophy. In my opinion, while those objections do put the central thesis of the paper into serious question, the young historian succeeded in pointing to the persistence of a certain ambivalent attitude toward the machine that is crucial to understanding the overall trend of the country's intellectual history.

☯

Mechano-finitism was indeed declared a heresy by the Church on the grounds that to regard the machine as a finite thing is to question the skill of its Creator. The machine, they claimed, was a divine gift of the Good Maker, the one and only perfect thing in the world, as the Creator is perfect. A major theologian of the era, in grappling with the philosophy's provocative idea in its own terms, asserted that the finitude of the machine's external shape is an illusion, as its infinity lies within. How else does it reveal new usage without end? To call it a mortal machine is to insult its immortal creator. In the persecution that followed, the proponents of Mechano-finitism suffered greatly, one of them made an example of by being burnt at the stake. But the movement introduced a powerful idea that could not be purged from the minds of intellectuals.

The nation then entered the age of absolute monarchs, who sought to centralize political authority and economic control over the land by radically curtailing the powers and privileges of the aristocrats and the priests. The latter were eventually stripped of their judicial license, while the scholars of the increasingly secular universities gained a great deal of influence in the court as they filled the ranks of the rapidly growing royal bureaucracy. It was in this intellectually freer atmosphere that Neo-mechano-finitism arose, suggesting a solution to the terrifying scenario of the machine's end. Mechano-finitism had demonstrated the finitude of the machine, the philosophers claimed, so we must prepare ourselves for the day it stops. We must build devices ourselves that can fulfill its many functions, and improve upon them until we are able to sustain ourselves when the machine ceases to work.

The beleaguered priests of the Church quickly pronounced Neo-mechano-finitism a heresy as well, asserting that to create devices that ape the machine is an act of sacrilege and ingratitude to its Creator. The machine was given to us as a great blessing, they said, so why insult the Provider by doubting it and trying to replace it with our own shabby and imperfect works? By this period in the nation's history, however, they lacked the political and legal authority to force their ideas on the people. And theology no longer provided the language of scholarly discourse in the universities. In the face of the great revolution in knowledge that followed, the priests retreated to the more modest task of taking care of the spiritual needs of their followers.

Neo-mechano-finitism became the intellectual basis upon which the new age of scientific inquiry and technological innovation was born. But what propelled it into its full industrial phase was a single volume of historico-mathematics. The greatest mathematical mind of the time examined all available historical records, looking at when new uses of the machine was found, and showing that the discoveries occurred at regular intervals of time. In addition to this momentous finding, he made the startling demonstration that the rate at which the discoveries were being made was slowing down at a regular pace. In other words, whereas the ancients found a previously unknown function of the machine once every few years, it took several decades for the moderns to do so. He came up with a mathematical formula that expressed the ideas, according to which an entire generation would miss out on finding a novel usage in less than a century.

This dry, complex work of historico-mathematics had a significant impact on the culture, as evidenced by the great variety of responses to it. Despite the fact that the machine showed no lessening in the efficacy with which it carried out its countless tasks, some thought that the work provided definitive proof of Mechano-finitism. They regarded the expanding gap of time between new discoveries as evidence of a depletion of energy in the machine. Surely when it has no more new use to reveal to us, they said, it will begin to wind down, ceasing to provide its services one by one until it becomes still and silent. Another major mathematician, however, argued against the notion by pointing out that the formula only demonstrates the indefinite increase of the time intervals and provides no proof of an end. He speculated that the proponents of the revised Neo-mechano-finitism were seduced by the narrative symmetry of their vision.

Certain priests of the Church of the Machine preached that the slowing down of discoveries was a warning from the Creator to desist from making devices that competed with the machine, even though the historico-mathematical work had shown that the process had been going on long before the Neo-mechano-finitist revolution. Interestingly, there was also a short-lived revival of traditional Mechano-rejectionism, its proponents seeing in the work's conclusion the revelation of the Evil Creator's design. Some of them followed the first Mechano-rejectionists' example by leaving the City of the Machine and the land, but few took that radical path.

The most important effect the historico-mathematical work had on the nation was a discernible acceleration in scientific and technological innovations, as scientists, engineers, and inventors worked under a new sense of urgency shared by the larger culture. In a sense, this development marked the ultimate triumph of Mechano-finitism as most citizens no longer regarded the machine as something that was unchanging and eternal, but as an object that was indeed a finite thing in the world. As devices of all kinds were made and put to work, taking on the many tasks of the machine, it became possible for the people to envision a future in which the machine would become superfluous.

☯

At a time when the industrialization of the nation was fully on the way, the most influential thinker of the day related, in the introduction to his first major work, how, as a young man, he had once struck up a conversation with a priest of the Church of the Machine who had attempted to persuade him of humanity's hubris in daring to ape the divine machine. "What the people of our time have forgotten," the priest had told him, "is that the machine is not just an object that does things. It is also an object that teaches. Why else would it be so beautiful, why else would its music be so sweet? Our ancestors first sat down before it, not because it was useful, but because it was a thing of beauty. And beauty was the first lesson that the machine taught them. It eventually taught them how to become a civilized people, and the Church was the vessel through which its teachings were transmitted. But now, in our heretic efforts to replace the machine, we have neglected to learn from it. Yet it teaches us still, and perhaps it will only be when it ceases to teach us that we will learn that we have lost something vital." Although the young intellectual had not been convinced by the idea, which he had known was based on misinterpretations of the historico-mathematical work, he had considered there to be a kernel of truth in his words. Perhaps the machine is a thing that teaches, he had thought, though not the lesson that the priest was thinking of. From this beginning, he built the grand philosophical system known as 'Mechano-objectivism' that featured an unifying explanation of all the branches of human knowledge with the machine as their central inspiration.

Despite the complexities of the ideas in his voluminous works, which addled the minds of many scholars, he became the most celebrated philosopher of the period for his explanation of the machine's nature that not only provided an optimistic vision of the future, but also celebrated the triumphant techno-scientific spirit of the time. Although he claimed that questions of the machine's origin and the identity of its creator were beyond the scope of his field, he thought that he had found its objective, not just in the nature of what it does, but how it has affected the civilization. It was indeed a teaching machine, he claimed, but one that taught the very opposite lesson from that which the priest had thought. "It wants us to ape its functions," he asserted at a public lecture. "It shows by example what things we must make to improve our nation. Its very objective is to guide us to a future in which we do not need it anymore. The closer we get to that future, the better we understand the machine. The slowing down of the rate with which it reveals new uses is a means of encouraging us. Have we not put so much effort into creating all the devices around us for the fear that the machine will come to a stop? But we should no longer do so out of fear, but in hopeful anticipation of the day when we reach self-sufficiency. On that day, I believe, the secret of the machine will finally be revealed to us." In his posthumously published memoirs, the lifelong agnostic allowed himself to conclude the account of his remarkable intellectual journey with a prophetic vision of humanity finally gaining total understanding of the machine's objective, being rewarded by it opening up to reveal its wondrous nature.

☯

A century later, as the negative effects of rampant industrialization became all too apparent, the culture came to doubt the philosophy's optimistic spirit. In this age of modernity when scholars began to question all received knowledge, the movement that was called 'Mechano-skepticism' began with a collection of papers by philosophers, scientists, and historians criticizing various aspects of Mechano-objectivism, and culminated in a series of conferences in which the system was taken apart, idea by idea. A historian of science, who became the leader of the movement, published a short work in which he compiled a list of unwarranted assumptions at the basis of the Mechano-objectivism and subjected each of them to rigorous analysis. Particularly devastating was his critique of the notion that, as we build more devices that fulfill the functions of the machine, we gain a greater understanding of the machine and that once we have built devices that can fulfill all the functions of the machine, we will have arrived at a perfect understanding of the machine. "Just because two things perform the same function," he pointed out, "does not mean that they operate under the same principles. Understanding the nature of one does not necessarily lead to understanding of the other. Even if we do reach the stage in technological development when the machine becomes superfluous, there is no reason to think that we will have learned a single thing about how the machine works. Imagine an artist who makes a statue of a woman he loves but cannot possess, and who believes that once he manages to create an exact representation of her, he will have created another her. That mad idea is at the heart of Mechano-objectivism." At a public debate with a staunch defender of the old philosophy, the Mechano-skeptic indulged in his famously vulgar humor, saying that the fact that he urinates does not mean that there is a cloud in his bladder.

Many adherents of Mechano-skepticism were those who were opposed primarily to industrialization. Some accused them of being secret adherents of the old-time orthodoxy of the Church of the Machine who hated modernity itself. Unlike modern devices, later Mechano-skeptics pointed out, the machine did not need to be fed with an endless supply of wood, coal, and oil; it did not ruin the natural environment with pollution and over-development; and it did not require armies of oppressed workers who are reduced to machines themselves.

The subsequent development of Radical Mechano-skepticism led to a bloody revolution, which was followed by an even bloodier reaction. One regime after another was toppled and erected, with more shedding of blood, until Social Reformism saved the day. After democracy was established and a compromise among the social classes was achieved, the scientists and engineers of the new era set about creating a new industrial system that was run in a more humane fashion and with technology that minimized its negative effect on the environment. In the new age of peace and prosperity, there finally came the day when the devices of the nation's creations fulfilled all of the functions of the machine, making it superfluous at last. And, according to the calculation of the formula in the historico-mathematical work, they would have to wait a full century before the machine would reveal a new use.

☯

A small group of scientists began to argue that since the nation did not need the machine any more, it was time they attempted to open it up, to find out once and for all how it worked and if it contained any clue as to its purpose and the identity of its creator. They were opposed by most scientific institutions whose members did not want to commit a reckless act with something they still did not understand. The 'Mechano-dismantlers,' as the former came to be called, accused them of cowardice unbecoming scientists and continued to make their case in universities, at public forums, and before the lawmakers of the land. The movement steadily gained supporters in the following decades, until it became a significant intellectual faction within the scientific and political establishment.

On the day the machine was supposed to reveal a new function, it failed to do so. The Mechano-dismantlers took the opportunity to claim that the machine had run out of uses and set about realizing their agenda. When they eventually succeeded in receiving the sanction of both the government and the central board of scientists, they took a high intensity energy beam device into the hall of the machine. They applied the beam to its immaculate surface for a few seconds, enough to drill a hole through any substance known in the world. When they stopped to examine its effect, they discovered only a tiny black spot. They considered the discoloration for a while and were about to resume the work, when a government official ran into the building, shouting at them to stop. A report had just reached the capital that the moment the experiment had begun, a far province of the country had disappeared into a vast blackness.

It was a great darkness of absolute presence that had swallowed entire cities and millions of citizens. Automatic probes lost radio contact the moment they went in and volunteers who bravely ventured into its perpetual night never returned. After much recriminations, the Mechano-dismantlers were dismissed from their professional and academic positions, and it was decided by both the political and scientific establishments that the machine had to be protected from further tinkering. A series of great vaults were built around the hall of the machine, making it the most secure and isolated location in the country. No one was allowed to come near it, and the decline of the nation began.

☯

As the country's civilization gradually crumbled, its citizens migrated out of the land in great droves. A century after the machine had been shut away, the first foreign explorers came to ascertain its existence, meeting along the way the very last people who were leaving the place. The explorers made their way through the vaults with heavy equipment and explosives, and when they finally managed to enter the inner sanctum, they found the machine intact and beautiful, still making its melancholy music. The visual tape they made of the excavation shows their leader noting the blackened spot on its glimmering surface and pointing it out to the camera. In the next second the music suddenly comes to an abrupt stop, and the machine vanishes into thin air.

☯

The descendants of the nation's citizens spread out across the world, moving far away from their ancestral homeland as if fleeing a place of bad memory. But whenever I encounter them, I am struck by the fact that they still talk endlessly about the machine among themselves, as if their ancestors' failure to solve its enigma put the curse of an obsession on them all. During the aforementioned conference I attended on the history of the country, I happened to sit during lunchtime next to a table occupied by three scholars who spoke in the near-dead language of the lost nation in a hushed tone. The conversation I overheard was so fascinating that I began to take notes on it, letting my meal grow cold.

This is a rough transcription of their exchange:

Scholar A: Another baseless assumption. Nobody knows if the disappearance of the province was caused by the experiment on the machine. It could have been a coincidence. A terrible disaster that happened to occur at the same time. A volcano might have exploded, or an eclipse might have taken place.

Scholar B: But a volcanic eruption and an eclipse are known phenomena in nature. The sudden appearance of a vast blackness is not.

Scholar A: They still should have ascertained if there was a connection. Apply the beam to another spot on the machine.

Scholar C: Oh, come now. Do you seriously think that they could have risked that? After an entire province was lost? One could forgive causing the first disaster because they did not know better, but a second one?

Scholar A: Well, we will never know.

Scholar B: We . . . they never did. But there's the world machine theory, which I've always liked.

Scholar C: Which theory is that?

Scholar B: The machine generated the entire country. It was the country itself. That's why it was so useful. That's why burning it with the beam took an entire province away. The machine stopped and disappeared when the nation ceased to be.

Scholar C: A machine for generating a country.

Scholar A: Powered by the people's desire for a civilization, for progress. Once they shut it away in vaults, they were cut off from it and lost that desire. So the country declined and died. Ironic how their desire to protect the nation by protecting the machine could have been the very cause of their downfall.

Scholar C: But what if . . . what if the experiment was a part of all that. A kind of a final test, perhaps?

Scholar B: What do you mean?

Scholar C: The province that disappeared. We cannot know for sure that it was destroyed.

Scholar A: No one returned from it.

Scholar C: So? Perhaps they did not return because they found themselves in such a wonderful state that they did not want to return.

Scholar B: What are you saying?

Scholar C: Perhaps the province was transported to a paradise as a result of the experiment on the machine. If the Mechano-objectivists were right and it was leading them to a goal, perhaps that was it. Dismantling the machine was the final thing they were suppose to do, which would have allowed the entire country to transcend to the next world. But as soon as the province disappeared, they assumed that it was destroyed, and took fright. So they failed the test. They could only go so far in their quest for knowledge.

Scholar A: Hmm . . . so we are not the survivors of the country's wreckage. We are those who got left behind. It was only the people of the province who made it to the world of the Creator.

Scholar B: They were the found, and we are the lost.

The scholars then fell into a deep, melancholy silence.

God having an understanding infinitely superior to that of man in extent, clearness and other excellencies, he may rationally be supposed to have framed so great an automaton as the world, and the subordinate engines comprised in it, for several ends and purposes, some of them relating chiefly to his corporeal and others to his rational creatures; of which ends he has vouchsafed to make some discoverable by our dim reason, but others are probably not to be penetrated by it but lie concealed in the deep abyss of his unfathomable wisdom.

—Robert Boyle, *A Free Enquiry into the Vulgarly Received Notion of Nature* (1686)

We are misled by considering any complicated machine as a single thing; in truth it is a city or a society, each member of which was bred truly after its kind.

—Samuel Butler, *Erewhon* (1872)

As he grew accustomed to the great gallery of machines, he began to feel the forty-foot dynamos as a moral force, much as the early Christians felt the Cross. The planet itself seemed less impressive, in its old-fashioned, deliberate, annual or daily revolution, than this huge wheel, revolving within arm's-length at some vertiginous speed, and barely murmuring—scarcely humming an audible warning to stand a hair's-breadth further for respect for power—while it would not wake the baby lying close against its frame. Before the end, one began to pray to it; inherited instinct taught the natural expression of man before a silent and infinite force.

—Henry Adams, *The Education of Henry Adams* (1918)

Perhaps universal history is the history of the diverse intonation of a few metaphors.

—Jorge Luis Borges, 'Pascal's Sphere' (1951)

. . . a novel, which is a machine for generating interpretations.

—Umberto Eco,
'Postscript to the Name of the Rose' (1983)

THE INFINITE CITY

> I, too, entered a city, I cannot remember when, and since then I have gone on, deeper and deeper into its streets.
>
> —Italo Calvino, *Invisible Cities*

When the ancient ruler of the Great Desert Empire finally succumbed to the fog of death, a controversy arose over the succession to the throne, as his only male child was not of his wife, but of his honored concubine, a foreign woman from a place no one in the land had even heard of, who just appeared one day at the side of the Emperor as if she had stepped out of a dream. The civil war that resulted raged across the burning earth for a decade, its extraordinary duration due in large part to the evenly matched cunning and courage demonstrated by the leaders of the two contending sides. The Golden Prince, the illegitimate but favored son of the old Emperor, commanded the imperial legions against a distant cousin he barely knew, the Red Prince who had been elected by the members of the Empress's clan and the disgruntled Lords of the Outer Provinces to lead their rebellion. As the years passed with the two men maneuvering their forces across the great gaming ground of the radiant desert, they became increasingly impressed by each other, not only for their skills as generals but also for their scrupulous adherence to the ancient laws of warfare. Throughout the duration of the conflict, both took care to minimize the hardship on the people and to treat prisoners with respect, severely punishing those who violated the rules of civilized conduct.

Ultimately, it was nature that defeated the Red Prince. A great plague wiped out his reserves at the fortresses of the Outer Provinces, and a freak sand storm devastated his best cavalry, not only ruining a brilliant flanking maneuver to capture the road to the Empire's capital, but also leaving the entire advanced line of his army exposed. The Golden Prince was quick to take advantage of the situation, and within a month he received news that his counterpart had been captured at a final stand of the rebellion. He was filled with mixed feelings, joy at his victory and regret at the end of the great game, as he awaited the transport of his defeated enemy.

The Red Prince, badly wounded during the last battle of the war, expected himself to be tortured to death in the dungeons of his victorious cousin's palace. He was surprised then to be greeted warmly by the Golden Prince who ordered his chains to be removed, refreshments to be brought, and his wounds to be attended to by court doctors. After he was allowed to rest and recover in the most comfortable fashion, the Golden Prince, soon to be the Golden Emperor, came to speak with him. He told the Red Prince of his great regard for him and how he considered it a tragic waste for the empire to lose such an intelligent and honorable man.

"The ancient laws dictate that I must execute you as the leader of renegades," the Golden Prince said. "But I am allowed some flexibility on the punishment if you are an immediate relation of mine." He proposed to the Red Prince that he swear an oath of blood brotherhood to him, and then subjugate himself as his bond servant for the penalty. If he should take the offer, the ruler promised to treat him with dignity.

The Red Prince was far from a coward who would try to save his life at any cost, but he too had come to admire his cousin and considered that he might have made a similar proposal if their positions had been reversed. He knew the Golden Prince to be a trustworthy man who would abide by his word, and thought that it would be a fine thing to be in the service of someone like him. He accepted the proposition and they soon became blood brothers.

The Red Prince was at his cousin's side when he ascended the Golden Throne of the Great Desert Empire and became his closest companion and advisor during his reign. They talked often of their war, aided historians in writing detailed and impartial account of its events, and continued their struggle for countless hours over the game board. Peace and prosperity prevailed over the empire, due not only to the wise and benevolent rule of the Golden Emperor but also to the fact that no one dared to challenge in war the united strength of the two most brilliant military commanders the land had ever known.

After the passage of years, when the emperor and his companion had become mature men, they were sitting over the game board to reenact a particularly complex battle they had fought in real life, when the Red Prince noticed that his sovereign was lost in some thought with a melancholy expression. When the former asked what troubled him, the ruler let out a deep sigh.

"These days, I am often haunted by a certain restlessness, a vague kind of longing for I know not what," the Emperor said.

The Red Prince considered his words and confessed that he too was visited by the same feeling.

"Through my rule and your advice, we have brought harmony to the empire, we have done our duty to our nation and our people," the Emperor said. "But we are warriors, you and I. We proved ourselves in the war, we made each other men in our struggles, and we conducted ourselves with honor throughout it all. But now, with all that we had to do achieved, we are becoming soft, our men are becoming soft, and we are facing the prospect of old age as soft men."

As they always spoke of what is in their hearts with utter frankness, they discussed their current condition and how they could remedy it. It was the Red Prince who suggested that they embark on a new project, a great task that would allow them to become what they once were.

"But where could we find such a task, when the empire is at peace and the people are content?" the Emperor asked.

"If no such project can be found in this world, Your Majesty," the Red Prince answered, "perhaps we can find it in the dream world."

He then related to the ruler how when he had been a child, he had once seen an old one-eyed storyteller at a market square and heard his tale. "Where the desert and the world of its great empire ends," he had said, "the dream world begins. A world filled with wonders that you can only catch glimpses of in your sleep. These are the fables of the dream world."

One of his stories had taken place in what he had called the Infinite City, a city without end, a city with no boundaries, a city that is everywhere and nowhere at the same time. The Red Prince had only a vague recollection of the tale itself, of a ruler who came to conquer the city but ended up being conquered by it. But he remembered how his dreams had been filled with images of the fantastic polis for months.

"But that is only a story, a figment of the old storyteller's imagination," the Emperor said.

"What if it is not, Your Majesty?" the Red Prince asked. "What if the Infinite City exists? Even after all these years, I can see the walls, the buildings and the citizens of the place so clearly in my mind, as if I had really been there instead of merely dreaming it. I know that there is a great market there, where they sell everything that you can possibly imagine. From the vast square of the marketplace, wide streets stretch out in every direction, as far as the eyes can see. I can picture it all right now."

"So it is from your childhood dreams that you believe in this Infinite City."

"Yes, Your Majesty. But then again, the great desert and the empire must end somewhere. Where it ends, what begins? Why do we have no answer to this? So, why could not the dream world be there?"

"The dream world, and the Infinite City," the Emperor mused. "It would be a grand thing if it did exist. To conquer the Infinite City. To conquer what is everywhere and nowhere at the same time. That is truly a wondrous thought."

Intrigued by the idea, the Emperor summoned the scholars of the palace and set them to the task of researching the legend of the Infinite City. After a time, they came to him with their assessment that it was in fact nothing but a fantastic story, but they did offer him scant evidence they had discovered relating to its actual location beyond the northern frontier of the great desert. Excited by the findings, the ruler and his advisor pored over the writings and discussed what little information they could garner from it. Although they had only vague suggestions of a possible northern route to the fabled city, they decided that a great expedition was in order.

After months of thorough preparations, the Emperor left a council of his most able ministers in charge of the government and led a great army of his finest legions into the north with the Red Prince at his side. The journey through the wastelands beyond the imperial frontier was long and uneventful, their greatest worry being how long their supplies would last, but just when grumbling began to be heard among the tired ranks of the soldiers, the advanced scout came riding back with exciting news. Only a few miles north, they had discovered a great golden wall that stretched east and west as far as they could see. They had found the Infinite City.

The Emperor and the Red Prince, accompanied only by a small group of his elite cavalrymen, raced ahead to ascertain the report. After only an hour of riding, they indeed saw the wall laid out all the way across the illuminated horizon, shimmering in its golden hue with such grand beauty that it made them doubt their eyes.

"Like the beginning of a dream," the Emperor commented.

"Or its ending, Your Majesty," the Red Prince said.

When the rest of the army caught up with them, the Emperor ordered his men to make camp and waited until the sun went down before sending his fastest riders to spy on the wall. They returned to report on a great gate straight ahead that was wide open, with a clear view of a bustling marketplace inside. The Emperor and the Red Prince spent most of the night organizing the final march to the city. The two of them, understandably, got little sleep, but when they dozed off for a brief time, they had an identical dream of themselves as old men, conversing and laughing over cool drinks in a drinking place. They were both soft and happy, free at last from the restlessness of warriors that compelled them to embark on the hard journey, but something about the image of them at the end of their lives disturbed the Emperor and the Red Prince so much that they did not mention it to each other when they awoke.

In the hour before dawn, the army gathered in tight formations before the view of the endless wall, everyone filled with great excitement at the prospects of witnessing the magical city at last. As the first ray of the sun lit up the world, the Emperor called out his order for the charge and led his cavalry at full speed. They raced to the golden wall and headed for the great gate of ornate design, still wide open with a marketplace beyond. The Emperor and the Red Prince let out war cries as they rode into the Infinite City.

They charged through the market, which the Red Prince recognized as the very one he had dreamt of as a child, across the vast square it occupied, and into a wide street that stretched into the city. Its citizens stopped for a moment to gaze indifferently at the invading army, but presently returned to their tasks. The Emperor and the Red Prince charged on with their weapons ready for combat, but no soldiers appeared to resist them. They rode on and on, until they realized that there was no end to the street.

After a while, the Emperor ordered his men to stop, and he turned around to look back. The advanced lines of his elite cavalry were with him, but the rest of the army seemed to have fallen behind since they were nowhere in sight.

"Perhaps they are trying to draw us in, Your Majesty," the Red Prince suggested.

"Yes. Let us pull back and regroup."

They turned around and rode back down the street and to the marketplace, but the army was not there. Furthermore, the endless golden wall and the gate they had come through were nowhere in sight.

"What on earth?" the Emperor said, looking around in confusion.

When the Red Prince rode up to a merchant at his stall and asked him the way to the gate that led out of the city, he was met with bewildered amusement.

"This is the Infinite City," the merchant said. "How can there be a gate out of it? If there is a gate out of it, then that's where the city would end, and if the city has an end, it wouldn't be infinite now, would it?"

"But did you not see us ride through here not long ago? A great army of us."

"I see many things here, both wondrous and ordinary. I see so many things that they blend together in time and meaning so that I cannot tell you whether I saw you and your army not long ago, or very long ago, or not all. That is the way things are here."

The horsemen searched the area for hours to no avail, many of them wandering into side streets and disappearing. When the Emperor realized what was happening, he summoned the rest of his men and ordered a count of their number. About two thirds of the elite cavalry were still together.

"Maps. We need to draw maps," the Emperor realized.

He divided the men into five groups, handed out paper and pens to their leaders, and instructed them to spread out in different directions while making detailed maps of the streets, with strict orders to stay together and return to the marketplace in exactly one hour. Although the group he and the Red Prince led tried to ride close, something about the nature of the labyrinthine streets made them lose half their men. When they returned to the starting point in an hour, none of the other groups was there, and they were uncertain if this was the same market they were in before, the map they had drawn so carefully making no sense. They awaited the others for hours, some of his men disappearing in the sprawl of the market in the blink of an eye, before they had to admit that either the others had gotten utterly lost or that they themselves were in the wrong place.

The Emperor and the Red Prince became thirsty so they went to a stall at a corner of the market to purchase some water. After they had their fill, they turned back to find the rest of their men gone.

"Have they been taken by invisible soldiers?" the Emperor wondered.

"Perhaps they are thinking the same thing about us, Your Majesty," the Red Prince answered.

They wandered through the market, looking around, and at some moment in the deepening day, the Emperor took a turn and suddenly found himself alone. He searched the whole night for any sign of his men, then the entirety of the following day. By the time night fell again, he became exhausted, so he found an inn where he rested.

The next day he searched, and went on searching in the following days, weeks and months, until he ran out of money. He sold off his trinkets, then parts of his armor, and finally his side weapons, until he was left with nothing but his clothes, boots, sword, and horse. One evening, after another fruitless day of the search, he became famished so he dismounted at one of countless, identical looking marketplaces of the city and went to a stall to buy himself a meal. After he had eaten, he was resting on a bench, fiddling with the very last coin in his possession, when he noticed a small crowd nearby gathering around an old one-eyed storyteller. As he began his tale, the Emperor listened with a vague sense of dread.

"The place that is called the Finite City," the storyteller began in a clear, hypnotic voice, "is bisected by a river that in the so-called 'radiant hour' at dawn, the rising sun illuminates in such a way as to turn it all silver. There is a modest wooden bridge over that river, and in the middle of the bridge, a large stone base for a statue. This is the story of that base, and why no statue stands upon it.

"There once lived a young girl in the Finite City, a humble person who had been abandoned as a baby on that very bridge at the place where the stone base now stands. She grew up to become a seamstress, but she also turned into the most beautiful girl the citizens had ever laid eyes on. Men from all over the city, even those of the richest and the noblest families, came to ask for her favors but she refused them all, as she was a modest and virtuous girl. One night, as she lay in bed, she heard the powerful voice of a mature man call to her in the darkness. She followed it out of her dwelling and walked the streets until she arrived at the bridge, just as the radiant hour came, the world around her turning silver from the glow of the river. In that moment, she had a powerful vision of a magnificent ruler in golden armor who identified himself as the Golden Emperor of the Great Desert Empire who had dreamt of her every night. He told her that because his wife was barren, he desired to take her as his honored concubine, to sire a son who would succeed him to the imperial throne. The girl hesitated over the offer, but was ultimately won over by the Emperor's kind expression and noble bearing. When she consented to be his, he smiled warmly and wrapped her in his radiance before possessing her. She woke up and found herself lying on the bridge, feeling herself a virgin no more.

"Months passed and it became clear that the girl was pregnant. When she was asked who had put her in that state, she spoke frankly of the Golden Emperor of the Great Desert Empire who had come to her from the dream world to make her his honored concubine. Some thought that she was simple minded enough to fall for a fantastic story some scoundrel had told her to dupe her into lying with him, others that she might have lost her mind after a rape. For the duration of her pregnancy, she had to endure the silent sneers and sometimes overt taunts of the citizens, her estimation among them having fallen from being a virtuous beauty to a possibly mad hussy. When she finally gave birth, however, the midwife was amazed to see that her child, a beautiful, healthy boy, had skin of pure gold.

"As the news spread of the wonder, citizens of the Finite City came in droves to see the child. The mother was happy to show them the boy at first, until she saw that the sight of his golden body was having a strange effect on them. Their interest became an obsession as people milled about outside her dwelling all day and night, refusing to leave even when she told them that the baby needed to rest. When she finally closed her doors on them and drew the curtains, they demanded with shouts and chants that she share her miracle with them. After another day of such incessant noise, she came out to implore them to go away, for the child was frightened by their screaming and could not sleep. But the mob refused to listen to her, continuing to ask for a glimpse of the child. She relented, hoping that one last viewing would satisfy them, but it only fueled their frenzy. Soon they began speaking of taking the child away from her and putting him under the care of the city so that everyone may bask in his glory. With the baby bawling in his crib and the people outside becoming crazed, she realized that she had to take her son out of the Finite City.

"In the darkness of the night, after the baby had finally fallen asleep with some cotton in his ears, she sneaked out of the back window with the child hidden in a basket. She headed down to the river, hoping to find a boat that would take them out of the city. Unfortunately, she was spotted by a man whose advance she had once spurned and who was still sore about it, who alerted the mob which came running and chased her onto the bridge. With a furious crowd blocking her escape at both ends, the mother grasped her child to her breasts, shaking with terror. As the people began to approach her with their fists and torches raised, she looked down at the golden face of her wondrous child and saw a serene, knowing smile on his face that told her what she must do. Everyone stopped in their tracks when she climbed onto the railings and gasped in amazement as she fell through the air and into the water with but a small splash. They ran down to the edge of the river and searched the opaque water, but the mother and child were nowhere to be found.

"The people remained standing around the bridge in shock, the guilt from their actions gripping their hearts. When the sun rose, and the radiant hour came, they saw tiny flakes of gold rise to the surface of the river, glimmering on the silver water. People went out on boats to gather the pieces, and after much discussion on how to atone for their collective sin, they decided to erect a statue in honor of the victims. An artist was commissioned to fashion the mother and child from the gold which turned out to be exactly the right amount for a life-sized image of them. When the work was done, they set the stone base on the bridge and placed the statue upon it.

"That night, all the citizens of the Finite City had a collective dream in which a magnificent ruler in golden armor came to the bridge on a great chariot. When he reached the statue, the image of the mother and child came alive and greeted the Golden Emperor with happy smiles. He helped them on to his vehicle and took them out of the Finite City in a blinding blaze of golden light. Next morning, the citizens came out of their houses to find the statue on the bridge gone, leaving only the stone base as the sole reminder of the wonder that had passed through their lives."

When the one-eyed storyteller finished the story, the Emperor became certain for some reason that he would never find his men or a way out of the Infinite City. As he also realized that he had to live on despite of it all, he went up to the old storyteller and gave him his last coin in the hope that the kindness would bring him some luck. With a heavy heart, he then went looking for a horse market to sell his beloved stallion.

He found the market and had a long conversation with a dealer who was impressed by his great knowledge of fine horses and offered him a job as an assessor. After some thought, the Emperor accepted. For the first year, he wandered about the city every night after work, hoping to run into his men, but he always returned home alone and dejected. After he became settled in his new life, he went out on the search less frequently, until he eventually stopped altogether.

He did well for himself as a horse merchant, becoming friends with his employer and colleagues whom he regaled with stories of his previous life as the ruler of the Great Desert Empire. They always listened to him with rapt attention, to his account of the long civil war he had fought against his cousin the Red Prince and of his great expedition to conquer the Infinite City, but he was uncertain if they took his tales to be true stories or fabulous inventions. He came to know his employer's daughter, an only child, and they fell in love. As her father had grown fond of his most competent and responsible employee with a noble bearing, he approved of the match and they were soon married. When the merchant became old, and it came time for him to retire, he handed the business over to his son-in-law. The former Emperor worked diligently, prospering until he became a rich man. His three sons and three daughters grew up, formed good marriages, and gave him numerous grandchildren.

Decades after he had first arrived at the Infinite City, he was getting on in his age and began contemplating retirement, as his oldest son seemed to be quite capable of managing the business without him. One evening, on his way home from work, he stopped by a local drinking place for a refreshment. As he sat back in a chair and enjoyed a cool drink, he noticed a man about his age staring at him from across the establishment. He stared back until he realized that it was his old companion and blood brother the Red Prince.

They exclaimed in surprise, embraced each other and even shed a few tears. When they finally sat down, they told each other of what had happened to them since they had been separated so many years ago. The Red Prince's tale was very much like that of the Emperor's, having gone into business after he had given up on his search, now settled with a family and a comfortable life. They avoided the subject of their failed conquest for a while, but finally spoke of it in a nostalgic manner. It was only then that they realized the true mystery of what had befallen them after they had entered the Infinite City.

"For a long time I considered that we all fell into a dream when we entered the city, Your Majesty," the Red Prince said, using the honorific despite the other's protest. "Once we were in the dream, in the dream world, of course there was no way out. This is the Infinite City."

"But now?"

"Well, now that I have lived half my life here, building my business, making friends, raising a family, I don't know what could be more real than this."

"Yes," the Emperor agreed. "I have felt the same way. When I look at my wife and children, I know that this is real. This has to be real, for I know my love for them is real."

"Exactly, Your Majesty. Which made me think that from the point of view of this world, it is the world of the desert that is the dream world. It is the desert that is everywhere and nowhere at the same time. All that emptiness, all those stretches of sand. Perhaps the empire and our previous lives in it were in a dream. A dream from which we awoke when we entered the Infinite City."

"The Great Desert Empire," the Emperor said in wonder, "all of its fortresses, its people, its legions, how long it has been since I gave a thought to any of that, since I wondered how they are now, who rules over them, what events have occurred there, how they speak of their Emperor and his blood brother the Red Prince who went on a great expedition, never to return. So far away and long ago. Yes, it does feel like it was all in a dream. Our war, how obsessed we were with it, even in peace," he said and they laughed in fond remembrance.

They shared memories until the evening deepened and it was time for them to return to their respective homes. Outside the drinking place, they made plans to meet again and embraced each other in farewell.

As the Emperor made his way up to the beautiful mansion on a hill that was his home, he could hear the laughter of his lovely grandchildren playing in the garden which filled him with a terrific sense of happiness. And it was through that pure joy in his heart that he finally understood that he had left the Great Desert Empire, journeyed across the radiant desert, and had come to this place, all in order to conquer the Infinite City, but in the end it was the Infinite City that had conquered him.

☯

That is the story an old one-eyed storyteller told a boy prince at a square of a marketplace. Upon its conclusion, the child's great aunt, the future wife of the golden ruler of the Great Desert Empire, gave the old man a coin and led the boy away. That night and for many nights afterward, the Prince of the Red Branch of the royal family of the Empire, became haunted by images of a city both magnificent and terrifying in its endlessness.

☯

> None is so disturbing as that of night DCII, magic among the nights. That is when the Sultan hears his own story from the Sultana's mouth. He hears the beginning of the story, which embraces all the other stories as well as—monstrously—itself. Does the reader perceive the unlimited possibilities of that interpolation, the curious danger—that the Sultana may persist and the Sultan, transfixed, will hear forever the truncated story of A Thousand and One Nights, now infinite and circular?
>
> —Jorge Luis Borges,
> 'Partial Enchantments of the Quixote'

II. FABLES OF THE DREAM WORLD

THE LOST PICTURES

The monk who woke in the forest of dreams had been an earnest servant of God before he was beguiled by profane love. He entered the monastery of his own accord when he was a youth, looking forward to a lifetime of service, fulfilling with humility and joy the modest earthly function God assigned him. Contentment in the house of the Lord was his for many years, until he was beset by an infatuation that was as vulgar as it was inescapable. The object of his tormented desire was the daughter of a merchant from a nearby town, a wisp of a girl who had only recently left childhood behind and who accompanied her father when he brought supplies to the monastery on his rickety cart. As soon as the monk understood the nature of his churning feelings, he withdrew into prayer, study, and self-flagellation, to save himself from the hellfire within. When none of that allowed him to forget the girl, and he found himself plotting to kidnap her, he became mad and fled the monastery in the middle of the night, weeping and cursing God for setting a test upon him that He knew he did not have the strength to endure.

For months the monk wandered from town to town, drunk most of the time for some relief from the agony of his heart, broken doubly by God and the phantom image of the girl. On a chilly autumn day, he was walking through an unfamiliar land when he was overcome by an exhaustion not unlike the shadow of death and lay down on the ground, hoping never to get up again. He slept a while, but was awakened by the cold and opened his eyes to see dark and twisted trees that surrounded him like so many accusing fingers. Beyond their angular shapes, the deep blue of the night was filled with the luminous eyes of stars. He lay still, staring back at them until hunger and the chill overcame his fatigue. As he got up and looked around, he saw that he was in a dark forest, on a narrow and meandering path. An owl hooted, a small furry creature darted by, and leaves whispered in the wind. He shakily got to his feet and looked around while rubbing at his arms, until he saw the tiniest flicker of light in the far distance. He began walking toward it without thinking, more from the habit of survival than any real desire to be saved.

The path led to a large clearing in the woods that was in the process of disappearing as tall grass and saplings overgrew it. In the middle of the open area was a large brown house going to ruin, with its stone walls cracked, its windows empty, and its front door smashed. The light came from a large lantern that stood before the gaping doorway, as if someone had stopped while about to enter the place and suddenly hurried away. The monk gazed at the strange sight, before the cold urged him towards the decrepit building.

He took the lantern and entered the house, not a little apprehensive at what he might find within. The hallway stank of wood rot and was completely empty except for great geometric swathes of spider webs, as were the adjoining rooms. It was only when he entered the largest chamber, at the back of the house, that he discerned strange shapes around him. He had the fearful impression of being surrounded by a silently standing crowd of people, but as he waved the lantern about to ward them off, he realized that the walls were covered with enormous paintings of vivid colors, so vast that the folk they portrayed were almost life-sized. And what paintings they were!

He knew little about art and what constitutes its greatness, but as he approached the pictures and studied their images, he had no doubt that he was in the presence of absolute perfection, the works of an artist divinely gifted. What made them so fascinating was not only the captivating way the subjects were depicted, but also the story they sequentially told. The pictures were eleven in number and set out the career of a great man.

The first picture showed the meeting of two men by a large twisted tree on an open field, beneath the fiery colored sky of dusk. One was a handsome youth, with dark curly hair and sharp eyes, dressed in clothes fine but worn. He was apparently an artist, as he held three brushes of various sizes in his right hand, and his shirt was marked with spots of paint. The expression on his face was serious as he pondered something with eyes cast down and a hand on the chin. Next to him was an older man dressed as a traveler, complete with a wide brimmed hat, a great leather coat, a black book under his left arm, and a short sword at his side for protection. With his right hand raised to the young man, the wanderer was talking with easy joviality. The shadow of the tree fell upon the traveler, obscuring his features, while the florid shades of twilight played wildly upon the young man, signifying perhaps his emotional turmoil. A far distance behind them was a large house with clean white walls, standing on the edge of a forest.

The second painting showed the scene of a great siege, in which the invading army had just broken through the gates of a fortress and was charging in as the hapless defenders scattered. At the head of the victorious force was a captain in glistening armor, recognizable as the young man from the first picture, who must have abandoned his artistic aspiration to become a commander. He was a brilliant sight as he held his sword aloft and inspired his men, even though he was bleeding from several wounds.

The third picture showed a grassy hill upon which a great crowd was gathered to watch the captain of the previous picture being knighted by an ancient monarch in a robe of red and gold. The sky above them was cloudy, but a single shaft of golden light shone down on the humbly kneeling form of the honored soldier, making him radiant as the sovereign who, supported on both sides by royal attendants, lay a great sword on his shoulder.

The fourth picture was of the victorious army's triumphant march through a wide street in a city of tall towers, greeted by throngs of joyous people. At the head of the grand procession were the monarch and the young knight, who had been granted the honor of riding next to his lord, both of them greeting the people with their arms raised. Upon the towers were comely ladies in colorful dresses gathered upon balconies, looking down at the heroes with welcoming smiles.

The fifth picture was a night scene in an enclosed garden below the walls of a mansion, where two lovers met in the generous light of a full moon. The man was unmistakably the knight, dressed now in a fine blue tunic, while the woman was the loveliest of the comely ladies from the previous picture, wrapped in a long, flowing dress of the purest white. The two held hands and gazed into each other's eyes, while a pair of playful servants watched them with glee from behind a bush, and an elderly lord and his lady looked down on them with approval from a window above.

The sixth picture was a marriage scene in a grand cathedral, where the lovers, dressed in brilliant hymeneal attire, were exchanging vows before a bishop. They were surrounded by friends and relatives, great lords and ladies all, gathered below a great stained glass window depicting the scene of the wedding at Cana.

The seventh picture showed a happy domestic scene in a sitting room, where the husband and wife stood together, holding and smiling down at a tiny infant wrapped in white cloth. Three older children, all handsome and healthy, stood at their feet, their arms raised in demand to see their new sibling.

The eighth picture was of a great hall in the shape of a vast dome, its wall lined with statues of great heroes and rulers, in which a crowd of dignified aristocrats was gathered, listening with rapt attention to the speech of the knight, now a mature statesman dressed in a somber black robe.

The ninth picture showed a country road where the nobleman, now an elderly patriarch wrapped in a green cloak, sat atop a white stallion, surrounded by farmers. As the people thronged about their lord with adoration, their master greeted them with an outstretched arm and a magnanimous expression.

The tenth picture was of an opulent funeral scene on a fine summer day, in which the nobleman lay on a bier, surrounded by a crowd of solemn mourners, from the grandest aristocrat to the humblest peasant, united in their sorrow at the passing of the good lord.

When the monk went up to the eleventh and last picture, he found that he stood before a mystery. He was immediately struck by its darkness and austerity which was in marked contrast to the brightness of the other paintings. It showed a large, dark chamber in which the ten previous paintings were laid out in order. Before them a gaunt and tired looking old man in a tattered cloak sat on a small stool, looking back at the monk with an expression of utter despair on his face. He was apparently the creator of the pictures, as his clothes were covered with paint spots and his hand held several brushes of different sizes. On the right side of the picture was a partially open door, through which fell the shadow of someone wearing a coat and a wide brimmed hat.

As the monk was completely puzzled by the meaning of this image, he looked back on the previous pictures to see how the last one might fit. He recognized certain motifs that he had not noticed before (for instance, the constant use of birds for allegorical purposes—a lone, proud eagle flying high in the cloudy sky in the second picture, a flock of doves released into the air by some children in the third, a tapestry with the image of a pelican stabbing its own breast to feed its young with drops of blood in the seventh, a robin with a worm in its mouth hovering above its nest in the ninth, and a dead canary in a cage, forgotten in a corner of the dark chamber in the last), but none of it provided a clue to the mystery. He walked before the great pictures for hours, until he grew exhausted and sat down before the first painting.

He remained still for a while as he gazed at the image of the young man and the elderly traveler conversing beneath a tree. Then he discerned something strange in the figure of the latter, which caused him to lean forward and inspect his form with greater care. It took him a moment to understand it, but when he finally did, he was filled with horror. Barely visible below the great leather coat, within the shadow of the tree, painted obscurely as if the artist himself was afraid to reveal it in light, the traveler's left leg unmistakably ended in a short wooden peg. As the monk searched through the other paintings, he saw the same man hiding in each of the following pictures—as a one-legged soldier here, a one-legged servant there, a one-legged peasant in another painting, and a one-legged nobleman in yet another. They were all the same person who, unlike the protagonist of the pictures, never grew old, remaining the same mature figure throughout the ages. It could only be concluded then that the traveler was none other than the Evil One himself—Satan, once called Lucifer until he rebelled against God and was cast out of heaven.

Now the meaning of the first picture was clear. The young man sold his soul to the devil, in exchange for which he embarked on a magnificent life, knowing every blessing, every glory, and every happiness on earth. The monk looked through the pictures yet again and witnessed all the success that came so easily to him, but always with the devil at his side. When he came to the last painting and examined the dark image of the old man again, he realized that he had been quite wrong, that the truth was even more fantastic and terrible.

After he had contemplated the face of the artist for a long moment, he became certain that he was none other than the young man of the first picture become old. In other words, he never became a knight, a father, or a lord. He remained an artist and a great one, thanks to the unholy gift bestowed on him by the devil for the price of his soul. He sat in his studio and painted his perfect pictures, one after another, until there were ten of them. At the end of this lifetime's labor, he looked upon the images he had created and realized that what he had portrayed was the life he could have had, had he remained true to the Faith and followed God. So he ended up an old man living alone in a dark house, with no one to appreciate his work. In despair, he painted the last picture exhibiting his fate, upon the completion of which the traveler returned to take him away forever.

The monk then realized that the house in the background of the first picture was the very house he was in now, in its better days before it became dilapidated and lost in the forest that grew around it, and he stood in the very chamber of the last picture. Stunned by the testimony of a damned soul that the images before him were, he sat down again and contemplated them. 'I must take these pictures out of this place,' it occurred to him. 'They must be shown to the world so that people may see their greatness and learn the terrible lesson in it.' After thinking on what he must do, he decided to spend the night there and wait for the new day to dawn, when he would carry them out of the forest.

As he felt overcome by fatigue, he lay down beside the heat of the lantern. He fell asleep right away, into a frantic dream of a sturdy door that he had to pass through but which would not open no matter how hard he pushed against it. After some immeasurable time in the dream, a terrifying knocking came from the other side of the door. As the heavy noise sounded again and again, growing louder each time, he took fright and ran from the pounding which pursued him into the darkness. The sound came down upon him and exploded right next to his ear, waking him from the dream to see the true cause of the wooden noise—the steps of a peg-leg traversing the room. He sprang up in terror and beheld a tall figure in a wide brimmed hat and a great leather coat pick up the lantern and fling it against the paintings, causing a great fiery explosion. The monk screamed and crawled away as the flames consumed the pictures in a matter of seconds and began to spread over the walls of the chamber. He somehow managed to get to his feet and run down the corridor as thick black smoke issued forth, filling the house and obscuring his vision. He ran on, until he became faint from taking in the foul fumes and soon felt himself fall.

When he regained consciousness, he found himself lying below a gray sky. He sat up and looked around, to see that he was on the side of a wide road that ran through a field of tall yellow grass with a small church in the distance. As he breathed in the crisp air, the sun made its appearance on the horizon, the first shaft of its golden light fanning out across the land. Just then bells began ringing from the church, the sound of which made him weep, first at the sadness of his fallen state and then in happiness for the certain knowledge that God had not abandoned him. The sun still rose, the world shone in beauty, and he was alive in His blessed world. As his thoughts turned to the house in the forest and the pictures it had contained, he understood what it all meant.

Once there was a young man who was destined to do great things in the world. Yet the devil came to him when he was still a youth and led him astray, making him a master artist in exchange for his soul. The Evil One allowed him to create his great paintings, but he also took everything from him, and finally showed him through his very works all that he had lost. The devil was triumphant and a lost soul descended into hell, but merciful God thought to preserve at least the lesson of his error by having one of His servants witness those pictures before they were destroyed. He could have sent a scholar of profound learning who would have fully understood the greatness of those paintings, or another artist with the talent to recreate them, or a great storyteller who could bring the pictures alive in his descriptions. 'Yet He sent me,' the monk thought, 'the humblest of His subjects who merely wanted to serve Him in what small way he could. This was an underserved honor, but He saw fit to grant it me so that I might know that even my life has its meaning in His vast and magnificent creation.' He then resolved to return to the monastery, to confess his sins to the abbot and to tell him of the wonder he had witnessed in the forest, so that the story of the lost pictures would spread and be known to all. Even though they were reduced to ashes and their creator languishes in hell, they would not have been painted in vain.

When his tears of happiness finally ceased, he got to his feet and made his way to the church. Upon his arrival, he knocked on its dark wooden door and was answered by an ancient priest with a bald head who looked at him with irritated suspicion.

"I was a monk who lost his faith, father," he told him in a steady voice, "but I have found it again."

The priest stared at him for a long moment before speaking in a crackling voice, like that of a furious crow. "You have been in the forest of dreams?"

The monk thought about the question, that was an accusation as well, before giving him the only answer that he could. "I must have, father," he told him. "I must have."

The priest waved for him to enter and led him into the church.

The monk spent the day and the night there, sharing modest meals with the priest who took care of him without uttering a word. He left the church early next morning to begin the long return journey.

☯

After a lifetime of good service to God, the monk, who became one of the most revered clergyman in the land, lay dying in the monastery where he had made his home since his return from the journey of his fall. With the final confession made and the last rites completed, there was nothing left for him to do but await his imminent end. He spent the last moment of his existence looking back on his life, considering his many experiences and achievements. Although he had done great things in the cause of true faith, he knew that he would be remembered as the protagonist of the story of the lost pictures that was well known across the land.

"But how do you know that the tale was true?" the voice of a mature man, perhaps that of a peg-legged traveler, suddenly whispered in his left ear. "Perhaps you fell asleep in a drunken stupor that night and dreamt the whole thing. Upon waking, you chose to believe it as real so that you could tell yourself that your insignificant life had its meaning in the endless, empty universe. The story was also a convenient one to tell your abbot when you returned to the monastery. It was God who had made it all happen, who caused you to fall for that girl, to flee the monastery, and become a drunk, just so that you might wander into the forest and witness the destruction of those paintings. With that wondrous tale, you received but a light penalty of penance before you were readmitted into the bosom of the church. But in the darkest moments of your meditation, it nagged at you that it might all have been a lie, a phantasm of your imagination, and that your entire life may have been based on an illusion. You must fear that as you cross to the other side, your Lord will come to you and say, 'Why have you spread a false tale among the faithful? Why should I allow a teller of falsehood into my kingdom?'"

'Oh have mercy,' the priest thought to himself. 'Do not sow the seeds of doubt in my heart now, when I am so close, so near to my Lord. Please spare me this test when I am at my weakest.'

"Doubt is an inescapable condition of this world," he heard another voice in his right ear this time, that of a young girl, like the daughter of a the town merchant he had fallen for so many years ago. "Yet do not fear your frailty too much, for you have been a faithful servant of God. What does it matter that it may have been a dream, when the tale taught a true lesson to the people and you have done good in the world. A dream may be a product of your imagination, but it may also be from elsewhere. Who is to say that even if the tale of the lost pictures were a dream, it was not God who granted that dream to you."

With those words, the abbot had a vision of that girl, not a day older, appear before him in a shining garment with a smile that was even brighter. She took his hand and lifted him from his deathbed and led him to a threshold. Yet even as he crossed it with a glad heart and peaceful mind, the tiniest fragment of doubt lingered in him like the shadow of a dissipating cloud.

LADY FARAWAY

The city at the edge of the dead plain was a lackluster place, as it featured no site of aesthetic or historical importance, but a steady of stream of travelers, especially those with a penchant for puzzles and marvels, visited it on account of the woman they called Lady Faraway. She was named that because she could only be seen far away, sitting somewhere upon the walls of the city, contemplating the empty world beyond with a sad expression. Because of her considerable and unchanging beauty, many young men throughout the ages tried to reach her, climbing over roofs and walls for days in order to ascertain that she was not some phantom of an ideal. Yet, even as they approached her still form, she would mysteriously be moved to a distance, never stirring from her position. Concerted efforts by groups of obsessed admirers came to nothing as her image always managed to elude them. During my brief stay in the city, I heard no less than five stories of who she was and how she came to be Lady Faraway.

The first story claimed that as beautiful as she was when seen from a distance, she was even more so at close range. In fact, she possessed beauty of such magnitude that every man who came near and beheld her, fell instantly and madly in love. When the fair girl that she was blossomed into a woman of perfection, she realized that she lived under a terrible curse, as her life became filled with endless admiration that often turned into desperate threats of kidnapping and rape. The distraught woman appealed to her guardian angel for deliverance from her unbearable condition, begging for the relief of homeliness. The angel wanted to help her without ruining God's workmanship of her form, a most magnificent demonstration of His art, so he turned her into Lady Faraway, still admired but at a safe distance.

The second story claimed that she was in reality a rather plain woman, who only seemed beautiful at a distance. The joke about her was that she was fair from afar but far from fair. As she was also extremely vain and became frustrated at having men chase after her, only to become disillusioned when they came near and turn away, she summoned the Devil, promising to give him her soul if he would make her the most admired woman in the city. The Evil One, being who he is, tricked her by making her Lady Faraway, indeed admired by all but because she can only be seen from far away.

The third story denied that she was or ever had been a real woman. Before the city was built, the site was originally occupied by four small villages that grew until they became interconnected. Their leaders eventually agreed to unite and form a single city, erecting a wall around it for protection from the marauders of the plain. When the work was completed, a serious disagreement arose as to where to put up the statue of the city's patron goddess, as it was believed that proximity to it brings fortune, and citizens from each of the original villages insisted that it be placed in their area. The issue threatened to lead to civil war, until a mysterious traveler appeared at the city's gate and offered a solution. The stranger, who some say was an ingenious craftsman and others a powerful magician, described a device that could move the statue around the city walls, away from the approach of people. The price he asked for its construction was exorbitant, but all saw it as an acceptable one for avoiding strife. After a time, the people became less superstitious and lost faith in the power of the statue, turning the image of the goddess into that of an earthly woman in their imagination.

The fourth story also denied the reality of the woman, claiming that she was a clever optical illusion created by the philosophers of the city to demonstrate the nature of truth for their students. "Truth is like a beautiful woman you can never catch up to, no matter how long you may chase after her," the greatest among the city's thinker once said, "but whose fairness keeps you in thrall, as you contemplate it from afar and sigh."

The fifth and final story I heard about the identity of Lady Faraway disclaimed the idea that she was an illusion, but also that she was a real woman living in the city. The strange mystics who lived as hermits outside the walls believed that it was the city that was unreal, that the woman was sitting somewhere in the real world, daydreaming of the place by the dead plain and the people who lived in it. The moment she is disturbed from her reverie and stops thinking of them, they said, the city and its citizens will all disappear without a trace.

THE WELL OF DREAMS

People made their journey to the well of dreams out of despair, seeking at least the relief of illusion from the weight of regret and sorrow. But before they could take a drink from the well, which would grant them a dream of their wish that night, they had to pay the old well-keeper who lived in a tiny shack by the well. What he demanded in payment was an object, whatever its worth, that was related to the dream each person desired to have. On the day I visited the site, three people had come to the place before me.

The first was a young woman who gave the well-keeper the dried leaves of a rose, the last gift from her lover who had left on a merchant ship, never to return. That night, she would have a dream of their reunion and a happy life together. The second was an old man, older than the well-keeper himself, who gave him a broken scepter from his earlier life as the tyrant of a vast empire. The people of his realm had revolted against his cruel and despotic rule, and had sent him away on a permanent exile. He would dream that night of the demise of his enemies, his triumphant return to power and perpetual reign as a god-emperor. The third was a prisoner in chains, brought to the well by a pair of militiamen for his last wish, as he was condemned to be executed the following day for the murder of his wife and brother. Driven mad by jealousy over his beautiful wife, he had become convinced that she was unfaithful to him with his brother, when they had merely been on friendly terms. He gave the well-keeper his wedding ring so that he might dream on his last night of their miraculous resurrection and a scene of reconciliation.

That night, as I sat in the well-keeper's shack, sharing a modest meal of rice and fish stew with him, amidst great piles of all manners of objects that were the payments for dreams, I asked the old man how he had come to be the well-keeper.

"I was once the poorest citizen of the nearby city at the foot of the desolate mountains, an orphan who lived in its rat infested slums," he told me. "I knew that I was the poorest because while every fellow orphan had at least one object to his name, I had nothing, not even a stitch of clothing on my back. One day, I was wandering out here, searching for a scrap of something to eat, when I came across the well, which was without a keeper then. As I had heard about the power of its water, I wished to have a dream of having one thing that I could call my own. And so the well became mine, and I became the well-keeper."

"So you got your dream for free," I pointed out, "whereas you charge everyone a price."

The old man chuckled. "No, my dream was not free. As it happens, I had to pay the highest price of all."

"What price is that?"

"The knowledge of whether I am truly living my life, or dreaming it. Every night I go to sleep in terror of the thought that I could wake up and find myself a destitute orphan once again. You cannot imagine what a torment that is."

I thought about that for a moment. "It is true that you cannot know whether you are dreaming this life, with myself as a mere figment of your imagination. But I myself know that I am real, and that this is not a dream. So, I know that yours is a happy story."

"How naive you are," the well-keeper said with a sardonic grin. "For all you know, you may be dreaming this moment yourself.

Perhaps you, a storyteller, came upon the well and wished to have a dream which you could shape into a story. Perhaps the well arranged it by having you share in my dream, that of an orphan boy lying somewhere, dreaming that he is an old well-keeper."

The old man let out a deep sigh before continuing. "The truth is, I envy you storytellers, for you have the ability to create something real out of dreams, whereas others wake up and can only despair at the loss of the world of their wish-fulfillment.

"If you should awake and find that all of this was indeed a dream, then I beg you to take pity on this orphan boy and give me another existence, if only in a modest story. Perhaps that will also be a way of defying the well itself, which I have come to believe is an evil demon that delights in the shattering of happy illusions."

THE DILEMMA OF THE KING AND THE BEGGAR

In the central square of the Republic's capital were two identical effigies, one hung upon a scaffold, the other enthroned. To explain their significance, our guide had to take us back to the days before the Revolution and the establishment of the Citizens' Republic.

The last king who ruled the nation became tormented by dreams of being the poorest beggar in his own realm, which he was subjected to every night. Unbeknownst to him, the poorest beggar in the kingdom dreamed every night of being the king. The monarch became incensed that with all his power, privilege, and wealth, he was obliged to spend half his life as his most humble subject, while the other became frustrated at having to wake every morning from the dream of royalty.

One day, the king was riding through the city when he came across the beggar and recognized him as the person of his dreams. He dismounted and approached the man in rags.

"Am I dreaming you, or are you dreaming me?" he asked the beggar.

"There is only one way to find out, Your Majesty," he replied before pulling out a knife.

As he plunged the blade into the king's heart, a royal bodyguard decapitated him with a single blow of his sword. In the next moment, the king woke up and found himself in his bedchamber, and the beggar in his hovel.

The king, after much thought on his condition, sneaked out of his palace at night and sought out the beggar.

"Look," he said to his poor counterpart, "as much as I wanted to avoid reaching this conclusion, it is obvious from our dreams that we are leading wrong lives. I was meant to be a beggar, and you the king, but we somehow ended up in each other's existence. So before this goes any further, we must exchange places."

As the beggar agreed readily, they took each other's clothes before one stole into the palace while the other settled himself in the hovel. On the following night, however, the beggar-who-became-the-king dreamt of being a beggar again while the king-who-became-a-beggar dreamt of being a king. Each of them had the same dream every night, so that nothing in their lives was changed despite the switch.

Eventually, the two of them came up with the only reasonable solution, which was to exchange places every month, on the night of the fullest moon. This did not make either of them happy, since whoever happened to be the king dreamt of being a beggar, and vice versa, but it gave them a sense of fairness from the symmetrical arrangement of misery.

When the Revolution erupted, the citizen soldiers stormed the palace to arrest the king, but found him gone. They caught up with him later that night, in the process of exchanging clothes with the beggar beneath a full moon. As the officers of the revolutionary army could not tell which one was the king and which the beggar, they put both of them under arrest. Their interrogation revealed that the two of them had been switching places for so many years now that they had honestly lost track of who had been the original king and who the beggar. This put the revolutionaries in a difficult situation since before they had set their plans in motion, they had agreed that as soon they succeeded in taking power, they would execute the king and raise the poorest beggar to the figurehead position of the People's Protector as symbolic acts of the old order turned upside down.

After mulling over the problem of the king and the beggar's forgotten identities, the revolutionary leaders sought the help of a dissident philosopher who had just been released from the former king's prison. The long-suffering Professor of Peculiar Metaphysics offered his solution thus:

"Your dilemma in the face of the identities of the king and the beggar arises from the mistaken assumption that you are dealing with only two people. In truth, there are two more beings whose actions and natures are directly responsible for both who these two individuals before us are and what they have done. There are the king-who-might-be-the-beggar and the beggar-who-might-be-the king, but there is also the writer of this very story that we are living in who created and wrote of these individuals, and the rest of us as well. But that is not all. There is also God who created the storyteller, and so is responsible for everything in the ultimate sense.

"Therefore, in order for you to enact the symbolic acts of executing the most powerful and raising the lowliest, you must look beyond these individuals, for they are mere shadows of their creators' ideas. The question you have to ask is who is the most powerful and who the weakest in the metaphysical sense. The only logical conclusion you can reach is that you must execute God, which is a perfectly appropriate gesture in the establishment of this Republic of Reason, and elevate his creation, namely the writer of this story we are in, to the status of the People's Protector. Of course, neither of them will oblige us by appearing among us personally, since the writer must write in his own world, and God must create in his, so we can only execute and raise them in effigy, which is most fitting for this nonexistent Citizens' Republic."

So the two individuals who were the king and the beggar, the beggar and the king, were released and paid off with a modest pension to disappear from history, while God and the writer of this story were respectively hanged and enthroned in identical effigies.

THE CITIES OF THE CHASM

For centuries, the people of the city speculated on whether the great chasm, at the edge of which their polis lay, was a blessing of the gods, keeping some unknown menace on the other side from endangering them, or a curse, cutting them off from some fortune or paradisiacal place on the far horizon. The only thing they knew for certain was that the chasm was bottomless, or so deep as to be that for all intents and purposes, and that it stretched endlessly north and south, as defeated explorers returned from their long journeys to report. Yet what kept the people fascinated by the unreachable world beyond was the vision that came to them once every year, on the first day of the worldly thaw, of a city on the other side that appeared for a single day, and then vanished into thin air. It was too far away to make out clearly, but all the citizens of the city came out of their homes and walked to the edge of the chasm to gaze at the distant walls and towers that resembled their own. Philosophers pondered its meaning, priests debated its religious significance; and scientists attempted to ascertain whether it was an actual city or an optical illusion. Artists made countless images of the place, while poets and novelists wrote fantastic tales that took place there.

The greatest inventor of the city, who had created countless useful devices and machines for its citizens, lost his wife and daughter to a plague, and resolved to leave the place as everything in it reminded him of his loved ones, cutting his heart anew with the blade of sorrow each time. Life held no more joy for him since his loss, so he made the solution of the mystery of the city across the chasm the last mission of his life. Working in complete secrecy, he constructed a giant balloon that would be filled with heated air and carry him across to the other side.

When the first day of the thaw arrived, he set off in his flying vehicle and flew over the city, to the amazement of the crowd that had gathered for the annual vision. About half way across the chasm, the inventor noticed in the distance another flying vehicle traversing the gap from the other side. Instead of a balloon, it was a great glider made of metal poles and sail, bearing a single person on the back of the wind. He soon lost sight of it, but had a distinct impression that it was heading toward his home city.

His balloon landed in a wide square of the city on the other side, and he was soon surrounded by its citizens. There were things in that place that he immediately found fantastic, such as the green hue of its people, as opposed to the blue of his own, the fact that mostly men seemed to be in positions of authority, not women as in his city, and that they worshipped the image of an eagle, and not that of an owl. He was eventually taken by armed men to a prison where he was questioned by numerous dignitaries. He answered all of their questions, and was able to learn that to these people his was the city that came to them as a vision once a year.

'Like the world in a mirror,' the inventor thought of the place, 'where I am right-handed instead of left, and it is the west window, not the east, that looks out to my garden.'

The dignitaries withdrew to discuss his arrival among themselves. A full day passed before they returned to inform him of their decision that his alien presence would prove too disruptive for their people. As they dared not kill him for the fear of bringing a curse down upon themselves for harming a stranger, he would have to spend the rest of his life in the prison. The citizens would speak of the blue man who came from the city on the other side of the chasm on a balloon, but in time, they hoped, it would become a mere rumor which would eventually fade into legend.

The dignitaries left then, and the inventor found himself alone in the cell that would be final home. 'I will languish here until I lose myself completely,' he thought in despair. 'And the memories of my past life will become nothing more than stories from an imaginary homeland.' But as he further contemplated his dark fate, his mind turned to that of the other traveler, the winged one he saw on his airborne journey.

'This world resembles mine, but is different,' he considered, 'so my counterpart may fare better in my city. Perhaps a woman inventor who lost her husband and son, who sought to solve the mystery of the city across the chasm as the last mission of her life. Perhaps she will be welcomed and embraced by the female rulers of my city and made a great heroine. And perhaps it will be through her that the enigma of our two cities will finally be understood.'

As darkness fell in his cell, and he huddled in his thin blanket against the cold, the inventor smiled in the first moment of joy he experienced since the death of his family. It came from the certainty that there was still hope for him, and for all the citizens of both cities. For it was hope that they had always gazed at across the darkest gap in the world, a hope that returned to them, when the tyranny of ice finally gave way to the new life of the sun's unending benevolence. And that, somehow, was enough for him to be at peace in that cold, dank prison, as he imagined his counterpart to be happy, in the warmth of his own home on the other side of the great chasm.

III. STORIES FROM AN IMAGINARY HOMELAND

A FEARFUL SYMMETRY

It is natural that I should have heard so many ghost stories while serving in the army of the Republic of Korea, at a base near the Demilitarized Zone, where the possibility of sudden death is a perpetual cloud hanging over everyday life. The tales ranged from the incidental (the night sentry's flashlight invariably turning off as he passes by a spot where a soldier died after stepping on a mine) to the extremely elaborate (on violated graves, wood spirits, a mad woman from a local village who disappeared into the hills after murdering her family, and headless spirits of soldiers who had slept during guard duty and were decapitated by North Koreans). The one that made the greatest impression on me is a handed-down story related to me by a corporal of a reconnaissance unit. It is but a trifle of a tale with a predictable moral, which I suspect to be a modern version of a traditional legend of local origin, yet I am drawn to the modest fable for what I might call its quality of symmetry.

Less than a month after I was promoted to private first class, I spent some time as a patient at a military hospital situated a few miles south of the corps headquarters responsible for coordinating the defense of the so-called 'central corridor' in eastern Gyeongi and western Gangwon provinces. The bed next to mine was occupied by Corporal An, a former professional baseball player who was suffering from a severe case of stomach ulcer. On a particularly humid July night, we found ourselves unable to fall asleep after lights-out, so we tried to forget our pains and homesickness by exchanging scary stories like children. Since I was the junior soldier, I went first by telling him the plot of a rather good horror movie I once saw on late night television, back in Los Angeles; back in my old life as a carefree graduate student spending leisurely days on Santa Monica beach reading Darkbloom novels and dreaming up stories instead of working on my dissertation. I managed to give An a good scare with a vivid narration, and then it was his turn to play the story-teller. He took a moment to gather his thoughts before telling me about a defunct guard post back at his base.

After An had completed basic training at Nonsan, he was sent up to the recon unit at the front, one of the toughest posts in the army. Late one night, his 'father' (in army lingo, a corporal assigned to a newly arrived private for orientation) woke him with a harsh slap to the forehead and told him to get ready for sentry duty. It was about ten minutes to two o'clock when they set out in the cold January night, shivering in the wind that pushed against their bodies and lashed at their exposed faces. The post they were assigned to was one of the farthest from the barracks, so they had to walk clear across the base, to an isolated corner at the southern end An had never been to before. The bunker itself was set below a low hill that looked down on a small village outside the barbed wires. After relieving the guards before them and taking up their positions behind the sandbags, An noticed a rectangular structure nearby that looked like another guard post. He wondered why there was one so close by, but he knew better than to speak to the Corporal before being spoken to.

Junior soldiers feared the hours of sentry duty at night as seniors often took advantage of the darkness and isolation to discipline them for infractions they may have committed earlier, or to harass them just to relieve boredom. A great deal of physical abuse occurred in those hours. An expected to be punished for having gotten into trouble that day with the company commander for failing to clean his rifle properly, but the Corporal, a former night-club bouncer who was given to pinching and twisting both ears until they burned, stood still and silent, seemingly preoccupied with his thoughts.

Time crawled at a maddeningly slow pace as the cold seeped into An's coat and fatigues before biting into his skin. He tried to forget the icy numbness spreading across his body by concentrating on the sound of the wind wailing through the trees. The piercing noise grated on his tired mind, but better this tedium, he told himself, than doing push-ups while being kicked in the head by his 'father.'

It was well into the second hour when he was startled by the Corporal suddenly stiffening and taking up his rifle before looking around the area. An himself tensed and searched for movement in the darkness but saw nothing. The invisible wind continued to howl in the night. A moment later An realized that within the sound of the wind was another noise, that of a woman weeping, coming from the other guard post.

"What is that?" he asked, his stomach tightening with the grip of fear.

"Be quiet," the Corporal hissed in a quivering voice.

It unnerved An even more to see that the tough Corporal was obviously frightened as well.

They stood stock still and listened to the uncanny lament for what seemed an eternity, until it gradually faded into the ordinary scream of the wind.

"What was that noise?" An asked again.

"I said shut up, you son of a bitch!" the Corporal spat out, embarrassed at having shown his fear.

The rest of the hour passed in fearful silence, until they were finally relieved by the next guards. They quickly made their way back to Operations where they reported to the officer on duty and returned to the barracks. After they put away their gear, the Corporal motioned for An to follow him into the bathroom. There they leaned against a radiator and smoked in silence, warming their bodies and settling down their nerves. The story the Corporal then told him had supposedly taken place several years before. When he himself had been a newly arrived private, he had heard it from a sergeant who had claimed to have known the people involved and had sworn that the tale was true.

There was a certain Sergeant Hong at the base who befriended a young woman named Miss Jin who worked as a waitress in the nearby village. It amused him to flirt with the innocent country girl who felt flattered to receive the attention of a college boy from Seoul, though he had only two months left in his service and had no intention of seeing her after he was discharged. One Sunday, he took a day pass and met the girl at a bar that evening after she got off from work. Hong got a bit drunk and asked Jin to accompany him to a motel. When she refused he became annoyed with what he took to be her coyness and pretended to walk off in a huff. The girl went after him, pleading for him to stop and let her explain. She told him that although she liked him very much she could not do as he asked because of a promise she had made to her father.

When the old widower had found out that he was dying of lung cancer, he had feared that his pretty daughter would become a prostitute like many poor and unprotected girls in the village near army bases. So on his deathbed, he had made her swear on her life that she would remain a virgin until she was married.

As Sergeant Hong still seemed upset, Miss Jin told him that she could make it up to him in another way. There was a girl she knew who had also dated a soldier at the base. Whenever her boyfriend had sentry duty at a certain post below a low hill near the village, he would give her a phone call and she would sneak over to him at the appointed hour with some rice wine and snacks. As she had told Miss Jin how to get into the place, she would do the same for Hong.

Toward the end of the following week, when Hong found out that he was assigned there, he called up Miss Jin who promised to come. Later that night, as he and a corporal named Min headed for the place, Hong told him about the girl. He was in a bad mood from having been harassed all day by the platoon commander, so he found himself getting upset all over again at her refusal to sleep with him. He told the Corporal what a teasing little bitch she was, and the conversation drifted to how the two of them would teach her a lesson that night.

Not long after they had occupied the post, Miss Jin arrived with rice wine and snacks. They did not speak much as she served them and they quickly drank down the liquor. When the two of them were sufficiently drunk they fell on her and took turns raping and beating her for the better part of an hour. When they were done, they sent the girl away, threatening that if she told anyone about what they had done they would find her and kill her. She went back to the village, to the tiny room at the back of a farm house where she lived. There, she cleaned herself thoroughly with ice cold water, put on her best dress and then hanged herself on a bare tree outside the house.

Three days later, soldiers standing guard at that post heard the crying of a woman in the night. One of them called out for her to identify herself but the lament continued. They then searched the area carefully but found nothing. They remained at the post for half an hour more, listening to the invisible weeper, before they finally lost their nerve and ran all the way back to Operations where they reported the incident. The same thing occurred almost every night. It got so bad that every soldier at the base was in dread of going to the place as even the most skeptical ones came back terrorized.

The regiment commander, Colonel Hwang, was visiting the base when he heard about the haunted guard post from a master sergeant of the unit. As the Colonel had a great aunt who had been a renowned shaman in Jeolla Province, he was open-minded about such stories and resolved to get to the bottom of it. That night, he and a captain accompanied the soldiers assigned to the place at the hour the crying was said to begin. They did not have to wait long before hearing the uncanny noise.

The Colonel, who had been instructed as a child on how to approach a ghost, walked alone into the night. In a calm and serious voice he asked whose spirit was there and what sorrow kept it in the living world. A moment later, the image of a young girl with a pale face and disheveled hair appeared before him, her eyes flowing with tears that streamed down to a ring of purple bruise around her neck. As he beheld the slight figure with her head bowed down and hands folded before her in a modest manner, his fear of the apparition was replaced by pity. The ghost spoke in a quiet voice without raising her head, telling him of who she had been in life. She told him of the promise she had made to her dying father, of Sergeant Hong who had befriended her, and of how he and Corporal Min had violated her, making it impossible for her to live on. When she fell silent, Colonel Hwang asked if bringing the wrongdoers to justice would satisfy her. She answered that that would allay her anger but not her sorrow, before dissolving into the darkness, the sound of her sobbing lingering in the darkness.

The following day, Colonel Hwang ordered an immediate investigation. Sergeant Hong and Corporal Min were quickly identified and put under arrest. Although Hong had only a month of service left, the stress from keeping the terrible secret had taken its toll on him and he confessed readily. The two of them were sent to the stockade where after three days they were found hanging in their cells.

When Corporal An finished the tale I was impressed by the neatness of the narrative but felt dissatisfied by what I initially perceived to be a flaw in its symmetry. A wrong committed was made right; a secret was brought to light; the victim's suicide by hanging led to the death of the perpetrators in the same manner; through supernatural means justice triumphed and balance was restored. The story should have ended there but it apparently did not. Soldiers continued to hear the ululation in the night, though An assured me that it was a rare occurrence now. But they still had to close down the guard post and build a new one nearby, the place where An himself heard the crying.

So the ghost was still not completely at peace, returning every once in a while to the place of her violation to grieve over what had happened there.

As I considered the story further, I thought of what she had told Colonel Hwang, that bringing the wrongdoers to justice would allay her anger but not her sorrow. It occurred to me that her sorrow must be not only from her terrible end but also the life she was deprived of when she killed herself. I thought then that perhaps what she may want, what it would take for her spirit to finally rest, was for her story to be written down, so that she might take on a new life, if only as a character in a story. I am forced then to come to the disturbing conclusion that she was ultimately crying for me, with Corporal An acting as her messenger. So on this dark, lonely night I find myself trying to relieve her sorrow by giving her an existence in a world of words.

And so I become a part, the final equation in the fearful symmetry of her tale, and you as well, as I imagine the ghost of Miss Jin becoming silent at last as she is reborn in your memory.

THE GHOST CHILD

The lovers sat in a darkened room, in the early summer heat that was enveloping all of Seoul, both knowing that the course of their affair was drawing to an end. The woman was content to let their last hours together pass in comforting silence, but the man wanted to tell her one last story, present her with one last mystery about himself that would ensure that she would never forget him.

"I want . . . I want to tell you something," he said. "A story. The strangest and the most frightening thing that ever happened to me."

"Okay," she said in an uncertain tone.

They sat in silence for a moment before he began slowly in a trembling voice. "After I was discharged from the Korean army, I went through a difficult period. Of course I was glad it was over. I was happy to leave the base, the barracks, the drills, and all the insane people there, but I felt no joy in the freedom. It felt strange, like I'd have to go back sooner or later because I belonged in that hellhole. For weeks, I kept dreaming about losing my rifle, getting punished by a senior, the Company Commander telling me I was going to the stockade, and so on. Even awake, I kept replaying some of the worst events in my mind over and over again. And I couldn't find the will to get on with my life. Going back to Europe, to the job at the Foundation, seemed pointless since I couldn't concentrate on anything. I felt completely drained emotionally.

"After a while, my parents started worrying about me. When I assured them that I just needed to rest, they suggested some things I could do to fill my time. My mother told me of a friend whose daughter had just graduated from high school and wanted to study in America. She had to take the TOEFL exam in only a few weeks, so her mother had asked if I could tutor her. I wasn't thrilled about the job itself but I thought I should pick myself up and do something, so I agreed to take it.

"My, uh, student, Mun Soyeong, she was a funny girl," he said with a smile. "When I went to her house for the first time, I found out that her mother had misrepresented her situation. She hadn't just graduated from high school, she had failed to get into the right universities two years in a row. And studying abroad was all her mother's idea. She thought it would be better for her daughter to attend an American university where she could learn English properly, rather than go to a mediocre college in Korea. Soyeong dutifully took the sample exams and memorized words, and I explained her mistakes and gave her tips on studying, but it was obvious that it was all a chore to her.

"On our third or fourth session, I noticed how bored she looked while I explained a paragraph from the reading comprehension section. I stopped and asked if she really wanted to do well in the exam. She seemed embarrassed as if I had caught her doing something wrong, and confessed that she had no intention of leaving Korea. She did not want to go to America, she hated studying English; all she wanted was to go to a regular university like all her friends. But her mother wanted her to know at least two foreign languages because she had a fantasy of marrying her off to a diplomat. Soyeong told me she was going to deliberately do badly on the exam so she couldn't possibly be accepted by an American university. She begged me not to tell her mother. I sympathized with her situation, but it put me in a difficult position. I didn't want to take her mother's money when nothing would come of the lessons, but

Soyeong implored me not to quit because that would make her suspicious, and she might also find another tutor who was not so understanding.

"The only solution I could think of was to go to her mother and tell her that I didn't know how much help I could be since there was only a short time left before the test. So I insisted that she pay me a lump sum after she received the result, and only if she was satisfied with it. She protested at first but I was adamant about it, so she relented and even complimented me for being such a scrupulously honest person. I didn't feel good about deceiving her, but I couldn't think of a better alternative.

"So I went over to the house twice a week, laid out the books on Soyeong's table, and chatted with her for an hour. She was an ordinary girl, but she had a sunny disposition I liked. After living with grim, harassed men for twenty-six months, she was pleasant company."

"Did you fall in love with her?" she asked.

He smiled ironically. "I wouldn't call it love. It was something . . . twisted."

"What do you mean?'

"It was like . . . she was a human sacrifice I had to make in order to get my life moving again. I began to feel a need for her, but it wasn't love or even affection. It was about how I could use her to help myself. I didn't plan on doing anything to her, but just the thoughts in my mind, of what I could do, how I could do it . . . they were disturbing enough." He paused for a moment.

"She, uhm . . . there was nothing special about her. She was attractive in a juvenile way and had a playful manner. She talked mostly about her friends, who among them liked whom, who was dating whom, who broke up with whom, and so on. She also told me all about her boyfriend, who was due to go into the navy. They were dating in secret because her mother had forbidden her to see him because he attended a mediocre university and came from a poor family. She wanted to spend as much time with him as possible before he was inducted. She planned to wait for him, but it concerned her that so many of her friends started dating other people while their boyfriends were in the military. She didn't think she could do that to him, but those girls had said the same thing until they met someone else. One of her closest friends sent a break-up letter to her boyfriend who was stationed at the front. He went AWOL and tried to come to Seoul, but was caught at a bus station and sent to the stockade. Soyeong told me that just the idea of her boyfriend getting into trouble like that made her want to cry.

"When the boyfriend went in for basic training, I had to console her during our fake study sessions. It become a little annoying, having to listen to her go on and on about how much she missed him, but a part of me saw it as an opportunity. One evening she called me at home. She was crying and seemed to be in a bad state, so I suggested we meet somewhere. We had some beers and talked. I did my best to cheer her up and then saw her home. After that we started meeting outside the sessions, mostly to talk, but then to the movies and once to a night club to dance. She told me how nice it was to have an older brother, which was a little unsettling.

"Then the TOEFL examination date came around and she jokingly asked me to wish her bad luck. She also wanted to buy me dinner for putting up with her all this time, so we decided to meet afterwards. I waited for her outside the university where she took the test and she came out grinning like a naughty girl. We went to a Chinese restaurant and then to a drinking place for beers. After we talked for a while, she became uncharacteristically serious and said how grateful she was for my taking care of her. She wished I really were her older brother so I'd be around all the time.

"She then told me how disappointed she was when she first met me. She was told I was the son of a diplomat who had lived all over the world and spoke English like a native, so she had expected a cool guy who wore fashionable clothes and drove an expensive foreign car. But I had turned out to be this strange, serious person who didn't even have a pager, who always dressed like he was going to a funeral, and was into all those complicated things like literature and history that gave her a headache. But then she realized I was just like that and that was all right with her. She only wished that I dressed better and let my hair grow out, instead of cropping it like I was still in the army.

"After that we went to a karaoke salon, sang and drank a lot, then I took her home. At her apartment complex, she wanted to rest before going in, so her face wouldn't look so flushed with alcohol. We sat down on a bench, and she was quiet for a while. She then began to talk about how her whole life was a lie. She loved her boyfriend and liked her friends, but sometimes didn't know what they meant to her. She didn't know how she was going to put up with her mother always trying to control her life and what would happen to her in the future. She began to cry, so I embraced her.

"She cried for a long time. When she calmed down at last, she looked up and smiled at me. I kissed her, first on the cheeks and forehead, then on her mouth. I kept kissing her even when I felt her become very still. I then touched her waist and then her breast, and she suddenly pushed me away. I looked at her, and found her looking at me with such anger on her face. In that moment, she realized what I had wanted all along, why I had spent all that time with her, why I had been so kind. I knew she felt betrayed. She hated me."

"I don't understand," she said. "Why would she hate you?"

He smiled weakly. "Soyeong and me, it was impossible. That was understood. She was almost ten years younger, the daughter of my mother's friend, she was my student, even though the sessions were fake. It was wrong in so many ways, and I crossed the line. The surrogate brother turned out to be a base opportunist.

"I tried to talk to her, to apologize, but she walked away without saying a word. I felt so ridiculous, I did not even go after her. Later on, I called her pager and left her a message, saying how sorry I was, how it was the result of momentary insanity. I asked her to call me but she never did."

The room darkened further with the evening's approach as he went on. "Needless to say, her mother never offered to pay me for the lessons," he said and laughed quietly. "But that sordid little story, it's just a prelude. The situation with Soyeong, it was a stupid mistake, but that . . . it took me to the ghost child."

"The ghost child?"

He stopped to think for a long moment.

"Not long after it ended with Soyeong, I got a call from my friend Sangjun, from the army base I served in. He was coming out on special leave because his older sister was getting married, and wanted to see me on his way down to Gwangju. We met at the railway station and had lunch. I was glad to see him and was interested to hear about everyone, but Sangjun could tell I was troubled. He asked if something was wrong, and I told him I had some personal problems I was trying to sort out. Then I said how nice it would be to get away from the city for a while, to go somewhere quiet to clear my head. Sangjun suggested I take a trip down to Cheonji, to the artists' retreat his parents ran in Jeolla Province. He could tell them about me when he saw them at the wedding, so they would expect me. I liked the idea, so I said I'd do it.

"A week later, I packed a bag and went to the railway station where I bought a ticket for the afternoon express train to Gwangju. I planned on spending a day there, then finding my way to Cheonji. As the train pulled away, racing out of the city and through the open countryside, I began to feel lighter. The compartment was almost empty so it was nice and quiet as well. I gazed at the view for hours, then took a nap. When I woke up, it was dark outside with only occasional dots of orange light in the night. Then I was startled to see that the seat opposite mine was occupied. A young woman in a bright red dress was examining me with calm curiosity, as if trying to remember where she had seen me before. She was pretty in the old fashioned way, pale and plump with thin eyes and tiny pouting lips in a perfectly round face. But she wore a vulgar little dress that exposed most of her pale chest and legs, that did not become her at all and was totally inappropriate for the season.

"She stared at me and asked if I was running away. After I thought about it, I answered 'Yes,' and she told me that it was impossible to run from oneself. We talked for a while and somehow got onto the topic of miracles. She asked me how far I would go to witness one. I replied that I didn't know, since I had little interest in such a thing. What if, she asked, someone told you that a miracle could be seen just around the corner? Would I go with him? I said 'Yes.' But what if that person told you it was over a hill, or at a neighboring city, or in a different country? How far would I go, how much trouble would I undertake for the mere possibility of seeing something truly wondrous? I told her I had no idea where I would draw the line.

"Then she asked, what if she promised such a sight, would I follow her to where she lived? I asked if it was in Gwangju and she said 'No,' she lived in a small village on the Western sea. I asked how far it was from the city. She told me I don't have to worry about that since the train stopped at a station that was half an hour's walk from the village. I said that was impossible since we are on an express train to the city. She smiled and assured me that the train would stop, it was just a question of whether I would disembark with her or not. It occurred to me that she might not be quite right in the head, but I decided to indulge her. I told her that if the train indeed stopped before it reached Gwangju, I would follow her. She smiled and turned to look out at the night.

"A moment later, the train came to a silent stop at an empty station without a light. I became confused and a little frightened by what was happening, but as the young woman reminded me of my promise, I had to follow her.

"We left the train and walked into the night, on a dirt road through the countryside. The only light was the moon, but it was bright enough to illuminate our way through the paddies. We did not speak as we eventually reached the end of the field and then climbed a low hill. When we reached the top of the incline, I saw the ocean and heard the whispers of the breaking waves. She led me down to a small village of tiny wooden houses, where all the inhabitants appeared to be asleep since the place was cast in complete darkness. She took me through a gate, into a small traditional house, slid open a screen door and went in. A moment later, she lit an oil lamp and bade me enter. The ondol floor was cold, but she told me that she would put the heat on right away and prepare dinner, and then left the room. I sat down and looked around the small space. All it contained was a large wooden chest with a pile of comforters on it. After a while, the floor began to grow pleasantly warm, and I found myself becoming quite relaxed.

"The young woman brought in a large table filled with a surprisingly extravagant feast of rice, fish stew, numerous side dishes, and liquor in a turquoise vase. She had also changed into a white hanbok dress, with her hair tied back and rolled up in the traditional manner. I was too amazed by the transformation to question her as she served me.

"I asked why she wasn't eating, but she merely averted her face with a smile. I ate and drank, everything was delicious, and I felt content. After I was full and just drunk enough to feel a pleasant buzz, she carried the table out of the room and returned a moment later with a bamboo flute. She played a few sad tunes that moved me, then went to the wooden chest and took down the comforters to lay them out on the floor. After she had arranged them neatly, she blew out the oil lamp. My eyes became used to the darkness, and I could see by the light of the moon shining through the screen doors, the young woman slowly taking the dress off. When she was completely naked, she undid her hair, and let it hang down. She then knelt down on the blankets and waited for me.

"I went to her as if in a trance and took off my own clothes with her help, and lay down with her. I kissed and touched her for a long time before mounting her. She was apparently a virgin, so it took some effort to take her, but once I was inside, she took the motions in stride and moved in rhythm with me. After I came to a conclusion, I lay down next to her, holding her in my arms.

"We lay still for a long time, feeling the warmth of our bodies, listening to our quiet breaths, and gazing at the bluish glow of the night. Then she began to speak, telling me the story of who she was.

"Her father was a humble fisherman, who was visiting the market in a neighboring town when he saw the daughter of a rich man and fell in love with her. He pursued and wooed her for months, until she too fell for him. When her family found out about the affair, they tried everything to separate them. The girl's father confined her in a room and hired thugs to beat up the fisherman. The situation reached a crisis when the girl took out a knife in front of her parents and threatened to stab herself if they did not let her marry him. As they could tell that she was deadly serious, they had to relent.

"Just after the marriage, the girl's father used his connections to get his son-in-law a place on a ship that was bound for a long-range fishing expedition that promised to be lucrative. His wife could stay at her parent's house while he was away. She begged her husband not to leave so soon after their marriage, but he knew that it was too good an opportunity. He consoled her by making a solemn promise to return in three months no matter what, on a winter day when they would meet at his house at the seaside village.

"After the months passed, the fisherman's wife went down to the port to meet the ship. She stayed there all day but it did not come. When night fell, she went to the fisherman's house and continued to wait for him. She fell asleep sometime in the night, but was awakened by the sound of the gate opening. Her husband came into the room, and she embraced him in joy. Although she noticed that he was rather distant and his body cold, she was too happy to question him. He calmly told her to lay out the blankets, and she complied happily. They made love, and she fell into a content sleep in his frigid arms.

"She woke up the next morning and found him gone. She got

dressed and searched the house, but he was nowhere to be found. When she returned to her parents' house, she found everyone in hysterics. Her mother told her the news that had arrived that morning of the ship having capsized in a storm, with no survivors. The woman thought the whole thing was a terrible misunderstanding, but could not speak of what she had experienced in the night.

"Several months later, when it became clear that she was pregnant, her parents took her to a doctor who told them when the baby was due. Since it was well after nine months following her husband's departure, they realized that she was with a bastard child. Her father became enraged by the dishonor she had brought on the family and beat her before throwing her out of the house. She went to the fishing village and moved into her husband's home, but the story of her infidelity soon reached the place and the people treated her with contempt. No one helped her or even talked to her during those difficult months, and it was only thanks to a stranger in a truck whom she happened to meet on the road that she could get to a hospital in time for the birth. A little girl was born, whom she named Haewol, sea moon, because the moon was full over the ocean on the night that she was conceived.

"Years passed and the baby grew up to be a smart and cheerful girl with an uncanny ability. One day, they were walking in the local market when they came across an old man who had always been kind to Haewol. When she saw him, she burst into tears and would not stop until he was no longer in sight. Her mother asked why she had cried, and she replied that it was because she would miss the old man. Next day, he was found dead from a heart attack in the night.

"On another day, the wife of the shop owner who lived across the alley from them was in hysterics because she had lost a gold ring, a family heirloom she had planned on using for her daughter's dowry. All the neighbors helped her look for it, but it was nowhere to be found. Then Haewol suddenly came up and told her that a rat had taken the ring and hidden it in a hole behind the rice chest in the storage room. Everyone thought that she was talking nonsense, but the woman was desperate enough to follow her directions, using an axe to hack at the wall behind the chest. She found a rat's lair there, and the ring. After that, the shop owner's family treated the girl and her mother with respect and the village regarded Haewol with awe.

"On yet another occasion, the fishermen were going to their ships early in the morning, when they found the girl standing at the pier. They asked what she was doing there, and she told them not to go out to the sea that day if they did not want to turn their wives into widows and make their children fatherless. They stared at her in astonishment but some of them laughed it off. As the sky was clear and it was high fishing season, arguments broke out among them about whether they should listen to the girl, who was already walking back to the village, having delivered her warning. As the fishermen were a superstitious lot, most decided to take the day off, but the more skeptical men ridiculed them and sailed out to sea. That afternoon, a freak storm hit the area, and the ships that went out were never heard from again.

"When Haewol was seven years old, a great aunt of her dead father happened to pass through the village. The old lady had no intention of seeing her grand nephew's faithless widow, but she ran across Haewol by chance and was astonished at the sight. She not only bore an unmistakable resemblance to her grand nephew, but she was the splitting image of her niece, the fisherman's mother, as a little girl. After she made sure of the girl's identity, she hurried to the neighboring town, to visit the parents of Haewol's mother. After the patriarch of the family heard the old lady out, he and his sons immediately set out for the house of the exiled daughter. When they saw the child's undeniable resemblance to her dead father, they realized that her mother had been faithful all along. Haewol's grandfather fell on his knees before his daughter and begged her to forgive him and come back to the house. So the mother and child moved out of the village and went to the family home.

"They lived there for three more years, until it came to the day exactly ten years by the lunar calendar after Haewol had been conceived. Very late that night, her mother came to her daughter and quietly woke her up. She told her that her father had appeared in a dream and said that he was coming for her that night. As spirits can return to the land of the living only once every ten years, and can take back one soul at a time, she had to go with him. She embraced her daughter and told her to be a good girl and to obey her grandparents well. She also promised that her father would come for her as well in another ten years. Haewol cried to be parted from her mother for so long, but she understood her words and bade her farewell. Her mother also shed many tears before leaving the room, never to be seen again.

"'And ten years has passed again,' the young woman told me, 'and I too had a dream of my father telling me that he would come for me tonight.' She was happy that she would be reunited with her parents, but regretted that she would go to the other side a virgin, without knowing what it is to have a husband. But then she realized she had some time left in the world, enough to find a man, if only for the single night.

"'And now that I am no longer a virgin and know what it is to be a woman," she said, 'I can go to the next world, without any regret.'

"As soon as she finished her story, I fell into a deep sleep. When I woke up suddenly in the night, I found myself alone in the room. I was seized by a terrible panic and got dressed, in a hurry to leave the place. I came out to the alley and headed toward the sound of the waves in the distance. I ran to the beach and saw her, the ghost child in the water.

"She was in her white hanbok, walking slowly through the water, toward a small wooden boat in the distance where a tall, mature man was waiting for her. At a far distance behind the boat, in the middle of the sea, was a large fishing ship, with a line of pale faces at its side. A full moon shone above them.

"I stood still, watching the uncanny scene until I found myself calling her. 'Haewol,' I shouted, and the ghost child stopped. She turned and looked at me with a surprised expression. I realized at that moment that I was not suppose to be able see what was happening. I was a man of the living world that she was leaving behind. I understood then that I too had crossed over in a sense, that I was only partly of this world. I was no longer just a man but also an unwilling psychopomp.

"Haewol looked at me for a long moment, but finally turned away. As I watched, she reached the boat and her father helped her in. He then rowed away, to the ghost ship. After the two of them climbed aboard, the ship sailed into the darkness, disappearing over the horizon buried in the night.

"After it was gone and there was nothing left to see, I sat down on the sand. The day broke not long after that, and I watched the dark blue of the sky turn gray. I sat still until I suddenly felt my body freezing. I went back to the village but found it empty of people. The houses, seen in light, were all broken down and decrepit, like no one had lived there for years. I looked around the place in a daze before I took the road back to the train station. After I came down from the low hill, I saw a small town in the distance, at the edge of the rice paddies, where I could see farmers already going to work. I felt extremely thirsty, so I walked to the place and went into a general store. An old woman was sitting at the counter watching television. As I bought a can of coffee, I asked her about the fishing village on the beach. She told me that a terrible storm had hit the place many years before, destroying most of the ships and houses, and the people had abandoned the place. No one had lived there since.

"The store was warm with a coal stove going, so I lingered there, drinking the warmed coffee at leisure. Then I heard the old woman say something in a pitying tone with her eyes fixed on the flickering screen. There was a news bulletin about the express train to Gwangju that I had been on, which had derailed in the night. They were still pulling out bodies from the wreckage with little hope of finding survivors. It was one of the worst train accidents in recent times.

"I would have been on that train, perhaps I would have been dead. Perhaps I was dead for a while. I don't know. Then I realized that I should call my parents, so they'd know I was safe."

At the conclusion of the story, the lovers sat still in the dark room, whiling away their last moments together in silent contemplation.

THE DEATH OF KING GONGMIN: A MURDER MYSTERY

The name of the country 'Korea' is a distortion of 'Goryeo,' the dynastic kingdom that ruled over the peninsula from 918 Common Era, when it was founded by the great unifier Wang Geon. In 1388, General Yi Seonggye defied the royal order to lead his army into Manchuria to challenge Ming China and returned to the capital in full force to begin his coup d'état. Four years later, he terminated the dynasty and ascended the throne as the first king of the new Joseon Kingdom.

☯

"You are writing in a foreign language for readers for whom all these stories are things that happened so far away, so long ago. Why are you telling the tale of an obscure king of an obscure age of an obscure country? What could you possibly hope to achieve?" the ghost of the dead king asked me in the impenetrable darkness.

I

For God's sake let us sit upon the ground
And tell sad stories of the death of kings

—Shakespeare, *Richard* II

The source of the account is far from reliable, as will be shown, but even there the mystery of the event can be discerned. One must read between the lines and ponder the inconsistencies and the inexplicable elements to recognize the six-hundred-year-old clues. The description of the murder and the investigation that followed is found in the 131st volume of Goryeosa (History of Goryeo), the 44th Book of Biographies, the 5th Section on the Lives of Traitors, in the Life of Hong Ryun.

On the 21st day of the 9th lunar month in the 23rd year of the reign of King Gongmin (1374 CE), at the royal palace in Songdo, the capital of the Kingdom of Goryeo, several men entered the King's private chamber in the middle of the night and butchered him with swords. At some point (it is unclear whether during or after the act), at least three people shouted, "enemy has entered," but the palace guards did not make a move for some reason. The royal servants, even after hearing (from whom?) that a terrible event had occurred, refused to come out of their rooms. After the murderers fled the scene, a court eunuch by the name of Yi Gangdal finally went into the chamber and found the place drenched in blood. He informed the others that the King is not feeling well before locking the doors. He then followed the King's order (Which King is being referred to here? The one he had just found dead? But the record states that the first sword blow of an assassin sent parts of his brain flying, so he could not possibly have been alive to give instructions. Was this an order he gave in advance? In other words, did he know he was going to be assassinated?) and gathered the high ministers Gyeong Buheung, Yi Inim, and An Sagi, and informed them of what had occurred. The three agreed to keep it a secret for the present so that they might capture the perpetrators as quickly as possible.

After they began questioning the royal attendants, they solved the case due to an incredible blunder by one of the murderers. Another eunuch by the name of Choe Mansaeng, a personal servant of the

King, was found wearing clothes stained with blood (He did not bother to change after the killing!). When he was put under interrogation, he told a rather sordid story of how he and five other men came to commit the crime. He named as his accomplices Hong Ryun, Han An, Gwon Jin, Hong Gwan, and O Seon, all members of the elite Jajewi ('Noble Youth Guards') who had been close companions of the King for the past two years.

☯

The description of the group can be found in the 43rd volume of Goryeosa, the 6th Book of King Gongmin, on the first day of the 10th lunar month in the 21st year of the reign of King Gongmin (1372).

☯

The ostensible purpose of Jajewi, which was instituted by the King himself, was the selection of the most promising sons of the nobility who would be instructed by the monarch himself to be groomed as the next generation of his most loyal ministers. The record, however, also tells a disturbing story of an entirely different objective. The King's much beloved first wife, the remarkable Mongolian Princess No Guk, died in 1365 in the process of giving birth to their stillborn child. The King became disconsolate over the death of his Queen who had saved his life two years before during Kim Yong's rebellion. As he became increasingly depressed, he left most of the state's affairs to his handpicked Prime Minister Plenipotentiary, the mysterious Buddhist monk Sin Don, to spend much of his time mourning at the Queen's grave and mumbling to her portrait that he himself had painted. Although he had two additional consorts and acquired two more after No Guk's death, he rarely visited them and was impotent besides.

In the entry for the first day of the 10th lunar month of 1372, the record states that the King finally went insane. Apparently the members of Jajewi were chosen not for their virtues but their youthful beauty and perverted dispositions. At night, the King would make himself up as a woman before calling young servant girls into his chamber. He would then leave the room and have the young men come in and engage in depraved acts with them while he spied on the scene from the next chamber. When he was sufficiently aroused, he would summon Hong Ryun and others to his bedroom and have sexual relations with them.

The record goes on to say that, as the King did not have an heir, he ordered the men to have relations with his consorts so that a male child could be produced that he could claim as his own. When consorts Jeong, Hae, and Sin refused by threatening to commit suicide if they were violated, he personally took several of the Jajewi men, including Hong Ryun and Han An, to the chamber of Consort Ik and ordered her to have sex with them. She refused at first but then the King threatened her with his sword which frightened her into complying. After this, the men often went to her chamber at night under the pretext of fulfilling the King's order to impregnate her.

It is written in the Life of Hong Ryun that two years later, on the night of the murder, the eunuch Choe Mansaeng was accompanying the King to the toilet when the former reported that he had just been to the chamber of Consort Ik and learned that she was in her fifth month of pregnancy. The King was greatly pleased by this and asked whom she had slept with. When he found out that it was Hong Ryun, he said that he would now have to kill him and the entire group of Jajewi men in order to keep the whole thing a secret. Then he added an incredible statement, "Since you know all about this as well," he told the eunuch, "you too will not escape death."

Choe Mansaeng, fearing for his life, met with the others he would name as his accomplices and told them of what the King had said. They waited until the monarch fell asleep, apparently in a drunken stupor, before going into his chamber and butchering him. And it was Choe himself who delivered the first fatal blow.

When the five Jajewi men were arrested and interrogated, three of them confessed to the crime, but Han An and O Seon maintained their innocence. It should be noted that the purpose of an official interrogation at the time was the extraction of confession rather than the determination of guilt, which was a foregone conclusion. Since those who did not cooperate were encouraged to do so by flogging their buttocks, tying their ankles and twisting them with a sharp stick, putting enormous weights on their laps, and applying heated irons on their backs, most of the questioned, guilty or not, ended up complying. It took great perseverance as well as a strong sense of righteousness to insist on one's innocence since punishment usually followed regardless of the testimony.

The penalty was swift and severe. At the end of the day, both Hong Ryun and Choe Mansaeng, the ringleaders, were quartered, while the other four men were hanged. The law also dictated that three generations of the family of a regicide had to be wiped out, so all of their fathers were imprisoned and their children were hanged. The wealth and property of the families were confiscated, and the wives were reduced to slavery. The brothers and uncles of the criminals were all flogged before being sent away in exile.

Two years later, in the second year of the reign of King U (1376), a legal problem arose concerning the punishment of the remaining members of the criminals' families. An official by the name of Yi Mubang went to the house of Minister Gyeong Buheung, one of the three investigators of the murder, and demanded to know why the properties of Han Bangsin and O Jin, fathers of the executed Han An and O Seon, had not been confiscated. The Minister replied that it was because their sons had never confessed to the crime during the interrogation. The official Yi countered that they had held out in order to avoid being executed as traitors, and since there was ample evidence of their guilt, there ought to be no more delays in punishing their fathers. Minister Gyeong made an uncomfortable expression and refused to reply, but eventually relented under the insistence of the zealous official.

After the properties of Han and O were confiscated, there was some question as to what to do with the other members of the criminals' families. Mercy was shown only to the wives who were allowed to live on as palace slaves, but the remaining fathers and brothers of the criminals were put to death while many of their other male relatives were sent away in exile. For the families of the ringleaders Hong Ryun and Choe Mansaeng, the punishment was extended even to their nephews, and even those who were initially exiled were eventually executed.

The first major inconsistency in the story can be found in the narrative of Prince U's ascendance to the throne, found in the 133rd volume of Goryeosa, the 44th Book of Biographies, the 1st Section on the Life of Sin U.

After the conclusion of the investigation, a power struggle took place in the court over the question of succession. Minister Gyeong Buheung and Lady Hong, the mother of the deceased King, favored selecting a suitable member of the royal family, while Minister Yi Inim, another investigator of the murder, favored the ten-year-old Prince U. The identity of the child who did become king is a difficult matter to unravel as the record tells a rather convoluted tale of the boy's origin.

In 1371, just after the Buddhist monk and Prime Minister Plenipotentiary Sin Don was ousted from power and sent away in exile, the King summoned his high ministers and announced that he had a male child by a slave girl named Ban Ya who had belonged to Sin Don. The boy, known as Prince Mo Nino at the time, was brought to the palace and placed with Lady Hong. The King then met with Minister Yi Inim and told him, "I no longer have a worry since I now have a son." He further explained that "I went to Sin Don's house because I heard that there was a pretty woman there who was fit to give birth to a child, so I became close to her and this baby was born." The obvious point of the announcement was the recognition of the child as his legitimate heir. There is, however, a complicated background to the story.

According to a rumor in the record, the slave girl was impregnated by Sin Don himself. When the monk found out about it, he sent her to the house of the mother of another monk by the name of Neung U, where she gave birth. But when the child died before it reached its hundredth day, Neung U, fearing Sin Don's anger, kept it a secret until he managed to replace the child with a stolen baby. A year later (1366), Sin Don, unaware of the subterfuge, brought the baby to his house and showed it to King Gongmin who had been concerned about his lack of an heir, a situation that was unlikely to change because of his impotence. The monk suggested he should claim the child as his own.

This contradicts the statement in the record of 1372 that the King had no heir. It also brings up the question of why two years after bringing the boy to the royal palace and pronouncing his legitimacy to his ministers, the King had the Jajewi men rape Consort Ik. What was the point of the atrocious bid to get her pregnant when he already had a male child that he had claimed as his own? The whole question of the boy's identity and origin is not a trivial matter since it goes to the heart of the reliability of the source.

☯

In order to understand why the narrative cannot be trusted entirely, one has to take into account the historical context of its production. In 1392, eighteen years after the death of King Gongmin, the Goryeo dynasty collapsed as General Yi Sungge completed his coup d'état of the kingdom by ascending the throne as the first king (r. 1392—1398) of the Joseon dynasty. In the tenth lunar month of the year, he ordered the writing of a comprehensive history of the previous dynasty. The man entrusted with the task was Jeong Dojeon (1337—1398), the main advisor to the monarch and the chief Confucian ideologue of the new kingdom. From 1394 to the following year, he and the historians under his charge completed Goryeo Guksa (National History of Goryeo) in 37 volumes. Four years later, Jeong was murdered by the King's ambitious fifth son Yi Bangwon who ascended the throne in 1400.

As Jeong's work then came under heavy criticism for its lack of objectivity, including an accusation that he had distorted the role of his own father in the foundation of the new dynasty to cast him in a favorable light, the King ordered a new work to be written in 1414. The project was placed under the charge of the former Prime Minister Ha Ryun (1347—1416) who was one of the most respected scholars of the time. With his sudden death two years later, the work was put in abeyance until 1419, in the first year of the reign of King Sejong the Great (r. 1418—1450) when its continuation was ordered. In 1442, Goryeosa Jeonmun (The Complete History of Goryeo) was completed, but six years later the King, a great scholar himself, discovered numerous mistakes in its account, including another attempt by one of the historians to portray his ancestors in an advantageous manner. He punished those responsible for the incompetent work and ordered a completely new work to be written in 1449, assigning two of his most trusted ministers, Kim Jongseo (1390—1453) and Jeong Inji (1396—1478), to oversee the project. The 139 volumes of Goryeosa (History of Goryeo) were finally completed in 1451, in the reign of King Munjong (r. 1450—1451). The work, along with the eighteen-volume Goryeosa Jeolyo (Abridged History of Goryeo) that was completed two years later, remains to this day the main source of knowledge on all thing Goryeo, as none of the earlier versions nor the raw materials (the Sillok—'veritable records'—of the royal court) that were used in writing the histories survived.

The main reason it took almost sixty years for the work to be completed is that the court historians who were compiling the history of the fallen dynasty were in a precarious position due to the political situation of the era. As they worked under the watchful eyes of the first kings of the new dynasty, they were compelled to portray the last kings of Goryeo in the worst possible light, to justify its destruction at the hands of Yi Seonggye. This is best exemplified by the question of King U's origin.

Most contemporary historians believed that the entire story of U being Sin Don's son (or that of some anonymous soldier according to the recorded rumor) was a fabrication concocted by early Joseon officials, including Jeong Dojeon who compiled the first history. After Yi Seonggye gained absolute power in 1388, Jeong was instrumental in convincing him to oust both the figurehead King U and, later, his son King Chang by claiming that neither had the legitimacy to be on the throne. That cleared the way for Yi to abolish the kingdom altogether and establish the new dynasty. In all probability U indeed was the son of King Gongmin by the unfortunate slave girl Ban Ya who was drowned in 1376 by the order of Minister Yi Inim after she went to Lady Hong and tearfully claimed that she was the boy-king's mother. Given the political climate at the time, it is impossible not to speculate on what other misinterpretations, slanders, and outright lies survived in the historical records through sixty years of almost continuous rewriting.

On the question of King Gongmin's murder, many later Joseon dynasty historians, including the great Han Chiyun (1765—1814), author of the 85 volume Haedong Yeoksa (History of Haedong—an ancient name for the nation), assumed that the crime was committed under the guidance of Minister Yi Inim himself, the investigator of the murder! They interpret the act as the ultimate bid by the conservative pro-Yuan (Mongolian) faction in the court to get rid of King Gongmin who was pro-Ming and a committed reformer. Although Han Chiyun does not cite any specific evidence in support of his theory, there is a cryptic passage in Goryeosa itself that lends support to the idea (the 125th volume, the 38th Book of Biographies, the 1st Section on the Lives of Renegades, the Life of Ji Yun).

Following the death of King Gongmin and the ascendance of U to the throne on the 9th lunar month of 1374, Minister Yi Inim, his advocate and protector, became the most powerful man in the Kingdom. With his allies Ji Yun, Im Gyeonmi, Yeom Heung, and Choe Yeong, the chief military commander of the nation, he quickly eliminated all of his enemies in the court through executions, exiles, and forced resignations, and reversed most of the previous King's reformist policies, including his pro-Ming, anti-Yuan stance. In early 1377, however, a conflict arose between Yi and his one time ally Ji Yun, who had obtained a high ministerial post in the 12th lunar month of the previous year. When Ji Yun failed to rally support from among the ministers and his fall became imminent, he made one last desperate attempt to protect himself by going straight to the King at the royal palace. When Ji saw that the thirteen-year-old monarch was in the company of his enemy Yi Inim and General Choe Yeong, an argument ensued which soon degenerated into a shouting match. During the exchange, Ji accused Yi of having had a part in the regicide since he and Hong Ryun (the ringleader of the assassins) were from in-law families. Apparently, Hong Ryun's father-in-law was a certain Yi Hwebi, whose exact identity I have been unable to determine but is presumably of the same Yi clan as Yi Inim. Ji Yun was subsequently dragged out of the palace and put under arrest. He was executed a few months later.

If the assassination of King Gongmin was a calculated political act, orchestrated by Yi Inim who covered his tracks by first assuming the role of the investigator of the deed he himself had organized and then speedily getting rid of the perpetrators who had acted under his orders, it puts the entire narrative of the murder as told in Goryeosa into doubt. Could it be that Jajewi was a legitimate organization created by the forward looking King and that all the stories of his perversions, as well as his ordering the men to rape his consorts, were baseless slander by early Joseon dynasty Confucian scholars who were out to portray the last Goryeo Kings as decadent and degenerate Buddhists?

☯

But the true mystery of the murder lies not in the contradictions, the inexplicable elements, nor the hidden agendas. It is in the context of what led up to the killing and in the consequences that followed. And the question of what really occurred can be answered only by a ghost, which is to say that they cannot be answered at all.

II

> History is after all nothing but a pack of tricks we play on the dead.
>
> —Voltaire

I imagine King Gongmin as a rather small, emaciated looking man in his mid-forties (he was forty-four at the time of his murder) with a long, angular face marked by protruding bones over hollow cheeks and thin, deeply set eyes with dark lines under them. His sparse hair is cropped short and half gray, as are his neatly trimmed beard and drooping moustache. I see him in a cramped artist's studio, drenched in the darkness of an absolute night, except for a single pillar of light that illuminates his bent figure and a large canvas set up on an easel, on which the dead monarch is painting with slow, graceful movements. He is wearing a thin black coat over a simple, loosely fitting shirt and pants of the same color. The picture he is working on is a contemporary version of Cheonsan Daeryeopdo, the fragment of the only extant work attributed to him (King Gongmin was reputed to be one of the great artists of the era). The two horsemen in Mongolian attire have been transformed into modern youths on motorcycles, but with the same shaved foreheads and ponytails.

I watch him paint in silence and wait for him to address me.

"So," he finally says in a tired voice without turning from his work, "What is your case going to be?"

I take a moment to gather my thoughts before answering him.

"Early thirteenth century," I begin, "a hundred years before you were born, Genghis Khan and his army of unified Mongolians rode into China. Beijing fell to him in 1215 and the northern Jin Empire was destroyed twenty years later. The first invasion of Goryeo occurred in 1231, the first of six expeditions into the peninsula which devastated the country. The kingdom held out for thirty years before capitulating around the time Kublai Khan became the master of the Eastern World. The penalties for resistance imposed on the country by the Mongolians were heavy, the northern third of the country as well as Jeju Island were annexed outright with a military base built at Ssangseong and an administrative center at Dongnyeong; an enormous tribute of treasures, livestock and thousands of women was to be paid every year; a government body known as Jeongdong Heseong, the Eastern Expedition Field Headquarters, was established at the capital, at first to organize the disastrous invasion of Japan that Goryeo was forced to take part in, then to serve as the Mongolian watchdog over the government; the court was forced not only to use the Mongolian language for official functions, but also to adopt Mongolian clothes and hairstyles; and the crown prince had to live in the imperial capital as a hostage and take a Mongolian princess for a wife. You yourself lived in Beijing from the age of twelve, until the death of King Chungjeong, your nephew, ten years later."

I pause to see if he wants to comment but he does not.

"In 1271, Kublai Khan established the Yuan dynasty and became its first emperor," I continue. "By the end of the decade, the Song Empire was taken as well, and so all of China and a substantial part of Eurasia were under his control. As for Goryeo, after the reigns of seven ineffectual kings who were the subjects of the Mongolian overlords, you ascended the throne in 1352. By that time the Yuan was in decline, the bickering imperial princes were threatened by the army of the awesome warlord Zhu Yuanzhang who would eventually drive them all out of China and become the first Ming Emperor in 1368. And you wisely allied yourself with the rising Ming star and forced the Mongolians out of Goryeo. You abolished Jeongdong Heseong, dismantled the military base at Ssangseong, took back all the annexed territories, and managed to repel a punitive expedition by the Yuan. The court also went back to using the native tongue and dressing in the native manner.

"The greatest problem you faced, however, was that much of the country was still under the control of pro-Yuan aristocrats, who had grown rich and powerful over the decades from their association with the overlords, including the relatives of Lady Gi, the Goryeo woman who had become a consort to the Mongolian Emperor. When you took them on directly by ousting them from the court and executing those who posed the greatest threat, they raised major rebellions on several occasions and came close to killing you, especially during Kim Yong's Rebellion of 1352 when you escaped death because of the courage of your wife, the Mongolian Princess No Guk, and because the rebels mistakenly killed a court eunuch who resembled you. Ultimately, you succeeded in getting the foreigners out of the country and in keeping the nation together through a series of internal conflicts and invasions by the Japanese Waegu pirates and the Red Turban bandits from Manchuria.

"But your most laudable achievement was the re-establishment in 1366 of Jeonmin Byeonjeong Dogam, the Directorate for the Reclassification of Farmland and Population, through which you had your Prime Minister Sin Don investigate injustices inflicted on the common people by nobility who had arbitrarily confiscated their property and sold many of them into slavery with complete impunity. Of course it was another way of attacking the pro-Yuan nobles, but you still did much good in freeing and restoring to the people what was stolen from them."

"If I was such a great king," he suddenly says, surprising me, "why am I universally regarded as a failure?"

I think about the question. There was not a hint of sadness or self-pity in his voice, just ironic curiosity.

"Your reformist policies did not last," I tell him. "But that wasn't really your fault. You were murdered. Then all of your policies were reversed by Minister Yi Inim. He stupidly went back to dealing with the Mongolians whose empire was breathing its last. Shundi, the last Emperor, was already preparing to return to the Mongolian steppes where his ancestors had come from. Even after the death of Yi Inim, Goryeo continued to oppose the Ming, which led directly to the dynasty's downfall."

"So everything would have been great if I had lived on."

"Goryeo might not have fallen at least."

"An unwarranted speculation. And you call yourself a historian," he says and laughs quietly. I laugh with him, but nervously.

"Yes, but most contemporary historians believe that you had the right policies in mind," I say. "You were a courageous and energetic ruler who took on difficult tasks during one of the most dangerous periods of the country's history. And what you and Sin Don did with Jeonmin Byeonjeong Dogam was a good thing by any standard of judgment."

"Sin Don."

"Yes."

"I suppose you have a way of explaining him as well."

He is right, but the blunt question makes me consider my ideas before answering him.

"I admit that he is the most mysterious figure in the whole story," I say. "He may have been the corrupt and avaricious Rasputin of Goryeo many people thought he was, or he may have been what the common people called him—a sung in, a sage and a holy man, a gift from Heaven."

"Or both."

"Goryeosa tends to take an overwhelmingly negative view of him, regarding him as a calculating opportunist from the very start. But you really can't trust Goryeosa when it comes to the portrayal of powerful Buddhists. Take the time when you first asked him to help you. The record of his life in the 132nd volume says that he pretended to refuse you at first in order to make even firmer your resolve to make use of him. I don't see how anyone can know such a thing about his motivation."

"Do you remember what he and I told each other then?"

"Yes. He said—'From what I have heard, the king and his ministers listen well to rumors and false accusations, but that must be avoided in order to bring well-being to the nation.' You then wrote him a note that said—'You, my teacher, will protect me and I will protect my teacher, so no matter what happens we will not listen to others or suspect each other. May the Buddha and the Lord of Heaven be witnesses to this.'"

"But I broke that promise," he tells me quietly, putting his brush down and looking into the darkness. "In the end I threw him to the dogs who wanted him."

"You may have had your reasons."

"I may have listened to the rumors and false accusations he warned me of."

"And there were plenty of those. But I really don't think that is the point."

"No?"

"The records say that Sin Don's mother was a slave woman, which is rather strange since there was a strict law at the time prohibiting the children of slaves from becoming monks. Historians have speculated that his father may have been someone very powerful to pull that off. Anyway, you had a dream in which someone came at you with a sword, but a monk appeared and saved your life. In 1358, when you first saw Sin Don, who came to you as a companion to a friend, you recognized him as the savior in the dream. You took him in as your personal spiritual advisor. After your wife died in 1365, you appointed him as your Prime Minister Plenipotentiary to handle most of the state's affairs. Some say that you did this because you were in a severe depression over the death of the Queen, others that the opposition to your reforms was becoming too dangerous, and you needed a complete outsider to carry out your policies. Perhaps he did become corrupt after that. Perhaps he was an influence peddler and a degenerate sensualist who liked to force helpless women to have sex with him. But again, I really don't think that is the point."

"What is the point then?"

"What he achieved. He was the one who personally operated the Jeonmin Byeonjung Dogam to free the slaves and return stolen property to the people. He was the one who managed to oust some of the most dangerous and conniving conservatives from the court. He was the one who took the criticisms and attacks for enacting your reforms. He was resolute and fearless. You chose the right person to act on your behalf. He served you well."

"Why did I send him away then?"

"I don't know. Perhaps he did become a monster in the end. Perhaps he did plan to kill you and become king himself, as he was accused. Or perhaps the pressure on you to get rid of him became too great. He was universally hated by the nobility who regarded him as a dangerous upstart who was out to destroy them. He had to be sacrificed for your reforms to continue."

"But what did that sacrifice amount to? Nothing of any significance was achieved after his death. And I myself was murdered only three years later. Since you seem to have a penchant for wild speculations, perhaps if I had kept my faith with him, he would have been there to stop the man with the sword from killing me."

I look at him to find a thin smile on his lips that unnerves me. We stare at each other for a moment.

"I want to ask you something," he finally says, looking down.

"Yes?"

"Why are you doing this?"

"Doing what?"

"This," he says with a graceful wave at the darkness around him. "You write in a foreign language for readers to whom all these stories are things that happened so far away, so long ago. Why are you telling the tale of an obscure king of an obscure age of an obscure country? What could you possibly hope to achieve?"

"Well, I," I mutter before pausing to think of a good answer.

"I think that yours is an interesting historical case," I say at last.

"Even if one looks only at your murder and its explanation, the primary documents say one thing, but the secondary and circumstantial evidences tell exactly the opposite story. You could very well have been one of the most unfairly maligned figure in the records."

"You are sure about that?"

"Fairly sure. I have played down the stories of your manic depression, sexual depravities and misplaced faith in certain people, but much of them can be put into doubt because of the unreliability of the source, and I truly believe that you were, in the final analysis, an intelligent, courageous, and benevolent ruler who deserves to be better known."

"I see," he says with a smile.

"Do you disagree with my interpretations?"

"I'm not here to agree or disagree, as you know, but I will tell you what I think. I think you need a hero, even a tragic one. Someone to justify your historical quest. But you know very well that every awful thing that has been written about me may be true."

"Perhaps, but the search for a hero is not my main motivation in writing about you."

"What then?"

"I first became interested in your story because of the mystery of the murder."

"Which you will never solve. You know that."

"Yes. But everyone loves a mystery," I say with a silly smile. He smiles back and even lets out a short laugh.

"That's not enough of a justification for all this, is it?" he points out.

"I suppose not. But there is something else."

"Well?"

"You. Here. Now."

"Ah."

"The mystery inherent in all history. How we can never know. Not really. And I think it's quite appropriate to use such an obscure figure as yourself for the purpose. I think that it would be absurd to do this with say, Julius Caesar or John F. Kennedy."

"That is why you put me in this place, in these ridiculous clothes and had me paint this ridiculous picture."

"Look, when I started doing the research, I thought I knew certain things that would allow me to see through the inconsistencies, the gaps, and the misinterpretations in the records."

"Like what?"

"Like my training as a historian and knowledge of the latest methodology of textual criticism that would allow me to take the narrative apart and expose the hidden forces at work. But then I realized that it wasn't so simple."

"Why not?"

"Because the more I went into the texts, the more I realized that I was dealing not with intellectual abstractions but real human beings. When I began to imagine their lives, their motivations and experiences, I was moved by their fates. Even the minor characters in the drama."

"Who, for instance?"

"Well, let's see . . . take Consort Ik. I know I'll never find out what really happened with the Jajewi men, if you really ordered them to rape her. But the record does say that they often went to her chamber under the pretext of fulfilling your order to impregnate her. Imagine what her life must have been like, a royal consort forced to suffer that violation over and over again for perhaps as long as two years. She did give birth, you know, to a girl. During King U's reign, his ministers, thinking that it was a boy, urged the ruler to kill the child. Although some of them tried to dissuade him from the course when the true gender of the baby became known, U ordered the execution anyway since the girl's existence was an evidence of his father's depravity. Consort Ik disappears from the record after that, but it is assumed that in 1394, two years after the fall of Goryeo, she was on the ship to Ganghwa Island, along with the remaining members of the former royal family. The vessel was deliberately capsized in the sea, killing all aboard. Just a few lines here and there in the records that tell the tragic life of this woman in the shadow of history."

"In the shadow of history..."

"Just like you."

"So," he says and changes his position in the seat, "you transformed these stories into a mystery tale, a tale without a denouement, in order to illustrate the enigma of history."

"Something like that."

He smiles at that and turns back to the painting. He looks at the work for a long moment before speaking again in a quiet but steady voice.

"I thought it might be something like that," he says. "Bringing up the dead, arranging them in whatever fashion you please, to tell the story you want to tell. But this has nothing to do with me. Nothing to do with poor Consort Ik, Sin Don, Yi Inim, any of us. It is all about you, once again. You, putting on a play with the dead, which is what all history is anyway. You find all kinds of things wrong with the record to make a hero out of me, you shift the characters around, you point out inconsistencies and create doubts, you suggest alternative scenarios, all in order to tell a tale of mystery. You say that you are moved by our fates, but I don't think that's true. I think you are moved by the music of your own imagination which you set to the uncertain fragments of the past which are all you have. That may be an interesting exercise for you, but for the actors themselves, to be a part of such a drama, that is like the ancient curse of wishing one to live in interesting times. How you use me, all of us, our sufferings, for your entertainment."

"Perhaps you are using me as well," I suggest. "The living using the dead, but history is also the dead using the living."

"For what purpose?"

"To tell your story. I may be wrong about you, about what happened on that autumn night over six centuries ago, but I know that at least a fragment of the truth is in there somewhere."

"And you believe in such a thing?"

"How can I not? It's important."

He suddenly laughs at that.

"An obscure king," he says, "of an obscure age of an obscure country. It appears that you are under a wishful delusion. No one cares, my dear historian, tales of real human beings or not. Even I don't care. I have no reason to use you. I have no interest in telling my story. I just want to get this over with and return to oblivion."

"I don't think you are being quite honest," I immediately point out.

"Why do you say that?" he asks me with a frown.

"Your portrait at the Temple of Kings."

He looks back at me and smiles in amusement.

"Ah, yes," he says but does not comment.

"In 1395," I say, "after the capital of the new kingdom was moved to Hanyang, today's Seoul, they started building the Temple of Kings to honor the previous rulers of the nation. During the construction, a freak wind blew into the site and sent your portrait flying into the air before falling on the floor with a thunder-like noise. It was such a strange occurrence that the officials present spoke of it as a sign of your spirit's discontent. After some discussion at the court over this matter, it was decided that a separate temple would be built to house the portrait in order to appease you. Similar stories were reported in other places as well, and in some parts of the southern provinces your image was worshipped as that of a god."

"I don't see why you brought all that up unless you actually believe in ghosts and spirits," he says with a broad smile. "What happened to all your Western education and historical method? A mystery tale, hero worship, now you are going to tell a story of the supernatural."

"But I already told the story."

"What story is that?"

"It begins with me looking at a ghost in an artist's studio, the ghost of a dead King who was murdered on one autumn night of 1374. An obscure king of an obscure age of an obscure country. A monarch in the shadow of history."

A CONFUCIAN COINCIDENCE

Sun Inho never had an occasion to concern himself with the nature of coincidence until he had an unsettling encounter during a brief visit to the bay area, a rather preposterous crossing of paths that occurred in flagrant defiance of space and time. As the plane he was on lifted off the runway and ascended over the wavy sprawl of San Francisco, he searched his mind for some notion of chance symmetry of events that could help him make sense of the events of the previous days. There were, of course, myriad ideas and beliefs that deny the reality of accidents, claiming that every occurrence in life fulfills a role in a larger scheme or a function in a system. What appears to be a coincidence is an occasion of special significance as it provides a glimpse into the hidden purpose or design. But Inho found such notions of little use as they required faith in an otherworldly reality or a systematic ideology he did not have. He was more attracted to ideas that preserve the concept of accident, but point to the aesthetic mystery of the event itself or to its didactic value in demonstrating how we naturally impose meaning where there is only chance, however fantastic in behavior.

The day after Inho arrived in the city, he expected to spend most of the day at the university. But his meeting with a professor to deliver a message from his patron ended quickly and he completed research at the library for his own work by the early afternoon. As he had a few hours to while away before meeting some friends for dinner, he strolled down Telegraph Avenue, trying a hotdog from a place of local fame, browsing in the street's numerous used bookstores, and observing the colorful crowd milling about. After about half an hour of wandering, he purchased a cup of tea at a generic coffee place and paused on the sidewalk to sip the drink near a group of young people who were chattering loudly about events from the previous weekend. His attention was drawn to an Asian woman among them, lithe and dressed in jeans and a white halter-top, listening with a smile to an excited narrative by a blonde in a leather jacket. Inho was admiring her long, shiny hair and the golden tan of her exposed back when her friend finished the story, making the others burst out in laughter. The Asian woman stepped back in merriment and suddenly faltered as the edge of the curb broke off. In a moment of terrible lucidity, he saw how she was going to fall into the street and get hit by a red car that was speeding toward her.

Without considering his actions, Inho dropped his drink and ran to the woman who was flailing her arms in search of balance. A second before she would have toppled to the ground, he launched himself onto her, grabbed her by the waist in a controlled collision and rolled with her off the lane as the car raced past them, screeching to a panicked stop. If there had been a car on the far lane, they would have been hit. They were lucky, then, to sprawl on the empty concrete with the woman's full weight falling on Inho, knocking the breath out of him. He was too dazed to understand much of what happened immediately afterward—the screaming of the woman's friends, a skinny man with thick, curly hair from the car asking if they were all right, and many arms helping the woman get to her feet, then him as well. They set him down on the edge of the sidewalk to recover.

It took a while for the world around him to return to its normal pace. After it was established that both the woman and Inho were all right, except for minor scratches, a policeman on a motorcycle appeared, and they pieced together what had happened. The broken curb was pointed out, and the man from the red car was found to be blameless, much to his relief. At further inquiries as to his well being, Inho stood up and showed that he could walk without a problem. The satisfied policeman left, then the man in the red car, and finally a small crowd of idle spectators.

"Wow," the young woman said to Inho as she came up to him, "I would have been mincemeat if it hadn't been for you. You saved my life!"

Inho did not know how to reply, so he merely nodded with a slight smile. She stared at him with large almond eyes.

"Was that yours?" she asked, pointing to the spilled cup of tea on the ground.

"Yes."

"Let me get you another one."

"It's fine."

"No, it's the least I can do," she said and turned to her friends. "Why don't you guys go ahead? I'll catch up with you after I buy Superman here a drink."

They laughed and made some jokes about the incident before arranging to meet later. As they began to walk away they said, 'Bye Superman,' to Inho.

The woman introduced herself as Julie Ryu and bought him a cup of tea and a latte for herself before they sat down at a table. In the course of the conversation that followed she was delighted to find out that he was Korean, as she was by ancestry, though she had been born and raised in Hawaii. She was also intrigued by his recent service in the Korean army and in his occupation as a historical researcher for an international foundation dedicated to the recovery of lost knowledge. He deliberately changed the subject before she could delve into that.

Inho asked about her background, and Julie told him about her father who had lived a typical immigrant success story, until he suddenly passed away two years ago from a massive stroke. He had come to Hawaii in the late 1950's, started out as a cabdriver, then bought a convenience store, worked day and night, bought more convenience stores, married a local Korean woman, had two sons and two daughters with her, went into real estate and made a fortune, sent his children off to top universities to become doctors and lawyers and professors, and finally died on his way home from a drinking binge with his business partners. Unlike her dutiful siblings, Julie, the youngest, had been the rebel of the family. Resenting her father's absolute authority at home, she had made a point of following her own desire by going to a university in California instead of the East Coast, and majoring in the non-practical subject of anthropology. When her father had died, however, she had been the hardest hit in the family and had taken a year off from school to stay in Honolulu with her mother to mourn with her. During that time, she had suddenly found all things Korean of interest, when she had been completely indifferent before. She had started taking a Korean language class that year, joined a Korean students' club, and planned to travel to the country for the first time the following summer.

"A friend I made through the club, she came to the States when she was like ten," she told Inho. "She's originally from Busan. Last year, she went back with her parents for the first time since they'd left, and she loved it. I can't go to my father's hometown because it's in North Korea, but I can stay with my mom's relatives in Seoul. I'm really looking forward to it."

"Where in the north did your father come from?" Inho asked.

"He said it's a place called Woldong. He never talked about it though."

Inho stared at her. "Woldong in Hamgyeong Province?"

"You know the place?"

"That's where my father's family came from."

"What?"

"It's a small town. They must have known each other."

Julie gaped at him. "You're just visiting here, you save my life, and our fathers just happen to come from the same little place in North Korea?"

They marveled at the discovery, but then it became time for both of them to go off to their respective engagements.

"So when are you leaving?" Julie asked as they came out of the establishment.

"The day after tomorrow."

"Do you have time tomorrow by any chance? I want to buy you lunch or dinner, whichever is convenient for you."

"You don't have to. I'm glad I was there to help."

"Well, that too. But actually I want to talk to you some more. I want to pick your brain about Korea. Considering the big coincidence about our fathers, there's got to be a reason we've met. Don't you think?"

Inho thought for a moment. "What's your father's name?"

"His Korean name? Seongnam Ryu. Ryu Seongnam, I mean."

"Ryu ja, Seong ja, Nam ja," Inho said in the most polite manner of giving the name of an elder, partly to teach her, but also to make sure he would remember it.

They agreed to meet for dinner the following evening and exchanged phone numbers, Inho giving her the one for his hotel room in San Francisco. As they were about to part, Julie stepped up to him and gave him a long, tight hug.

"Thanks for saving my life," she said with a bright, childlike smile that moved him.

Inho had a long, jovial night with his friends in the city and returned to the hotel a little drunk. As he lay down on the bed and went over the events of the day, he found himself thinking about Julie. After resting for a bit, he went into the bathroom and took a shower to wake himself up. He then picked up the phone and called his parents' home in Seoul.

His mother answered and was pleasantly surprised to hear from him, as he had called only a few days before. He gave her a brief account of his latest activities and inquired after theirs, before asking to speak to his father.

"I met someone today whose father is originally from Woldong," Inho said after greeting him.

"Is that so? What is the name of the person?"

"Ryu Seongnam."

A moment of silence passed.

"Did you know him?" Inho asked expectantly.

"Yes," he answered, his voice thick with memory. "I did not know him well, he was much younger than I, but his father . . . he worked at our family orchard."

"Is that so?" Inho said in surprise.

"After the war . . . his son emigrated to Hawaii. Is he still there?"

"He died two years ago."

"The poor man. Your grandfather felt so guilty toward him."

"Why?"

His father let out a deep sigh as a prelude to revealing the enormity of the coincidence of his meeting Julie Ryu, the daughter of Ryu Seongnam.

The following evening, Inho met Julie at an upscale Italian restaurant on Market Street, a fitting place as it had all kinds of significance for Inho that he himself could not fully appreciate.

"Let me ask you something," he said over dessert. "You said your father did not speak about his hometown. About Woldong. Did you wonder about that?"

Julie nodded, shining brightly and darkly at the same time with her tanned body sheathed in a bright white dress. "When I was going through my rebellious phase in high school, I sort of knew he didn't want to talk about it, so I bugged him about it. I kept asking him what the place was like, what he did there and so on, he lost his temper and screamed at me to shut up. Once I screamed back and he slapped me."

"Was it only about provoking him?"

Julie thought. "Mostly. But I was curious too. Mom once told me that I shouldn't ask him about his past in Korea because something bad probably happened there, so I wanted to know too."

Inho frowned and took a sip of wine.

"Why? What is it?" Julie asked.

"I called my father last night. He used to know him."

"Really?"

"Your grandfather worked at an orchard our family had there."

"Oh wow."

"And your mother was right. Something bad did happen. You know, it's quite mind boggling that we've met like this."

Julie looked down and thought for a moment. "Is this . . . is what happened there . . . do you think that explains why he was like that?"

"What was he like?"

"So bitter and angry all the time. He could never just enjoy his life, his wealth, because he thought it could all be taken away from him at any time. He used to tell us that we can never be real Americans because they, even our friends and teachers, look down on us and will try to get rid of us unless we work twice as hard and are twice as smart as they are. He thought I was stupid for refusing to be as bitter as he was."

"I don't know."

"Do I want to hear this story?"

Inho thought about the question but could not find an answer.

"I don't think I want to know," she said. "But I guess I should hear it."

☯

According to the Sun family's jokbo, the book of clan genealogy, the line was originally of the noble yangban stock, with the names of several ministers and generals from it appearing in the royal records of early Joseon dynasty. The family, however, lost its status in the late fifteenth century, when its patriarch, Inho's direct ancestor, who had been a senior scholar in the Royal Historical Office, was exiled to the northern province during the purging of scholars by the mad king who would be called Prince Yeonsan because he was finally deposed and so never given an honorific temple name at his death. The patriarch was vindicated in the reign of King Jungjong, but by that time he was too old and sickly to return to the capital, and the family settled down permanently in the village of Woldong. The property there had once been significant, but it dwindled over the centuries and all that was left by the Japanese colonization of 1910 was a modest orchard that grew apples. The only signs that remained of the family's noble origin were the literacy of its males, as an older member operated the local school, and the family patriarch's traditional position as the village headman. Inho's great-grandfather was once jailed and beaten by Japanese policemen after he was caught teaching the native script, which had become forbidden. Other than that, the family went through the colonial era without too much suffering.

After the Japanese left in 1945, Inho's grandfather, an ambitious man who had studied economics at a university in Japan, took over the management of the family estate for his bedridden father. He had plans to expand the property and turn the local school into a proper modern elementary school. In 1947 he sent his oldest son, Inho's father, to live with maternal relatives in Pyongyang so he could attend the newly established Kim Ilsung University.

"Your grandfather was one of six people who worked at the orchard," Inho told Julie.

"Was this when Korea was divided?" Julie asked.

"The two countries didn't become officially independent until 1948, but the border was drawn, and the Soviet occupation force was helping Kim Ilsung set up the communist state."

"They must have taken away the property," Julie said, showing that she knew something about the history.

"Not right away. In countries that were still largely pre-industrial, they implemented communism in stages. The first thing they did was to enact what they called comprehensive land reform. The party official who was in charge of the district's People's Committee, he had been an officer in Kim Ilsung's guerilla unit during the war and was apparently a real zealot. My father remembers his name only because he had one of those rare two syllable family names—Dokgo. Comrade Dokgo Hyoseok. He and a group of party officials came to the village and announced that all property would be divided equally among people who actually worked the land. That put an end to my grandfather's expansion plan, but he managed not to lose everything by convincing the officials that although his family owned the land, they also labored on the property themselves. So the orchard was cut up into seven pieces, only one of which remained in the family. The workers liked it, of course, since they suddenly became property owners. But most of them had always gotten along well with our family, so they tried not to seem too pleased. Except . . . well, except your grandfather."

"What . . . oh. What did he . . . "

Inho considered his answer for a moment. "Look, all of this is subjective. My father wasn't even in Woldong at the time, so most of this is what he heard from his father."

"Okay," she said.

"Apparently, your grandfather was a bit of a malcontent. He complained constantly about the work and got into feuds with other workers. It wasn't easy work by any means, so I'm sure he had his reasons."

"I get it," Julie said with an indulgent smile, amused by his show of fairness.

"Anyway," he said, smiling back, "when the land reform was enacted, he went on a celebratory binge. That night, he came to the family house drunk and began screaming about how he didn't have to take orders anymore, how a new world had arrived and how he was going to make his own way in it and show all the snobs who was better. Finally, three other workers who happened to be there, they had to drag him away, kicking and yelling.

"In the following days, the workers, who were now part owners, continued to show their respect to my grandfather and the family, but your grandfather would make a point of ignoring them or making comments like, 'How fine this new world is, where there are no landlords. No rich, no poor, where everyone is equal and owns things equally. How nice it is to live to see such a world.'"

"Why did he leave if it was so nice?"

"Because it soon became apparent that the new system wasn't all it was cracked up to be." Inho paused for a moment to think. "Years ago, when I asked my father what made him take his family and leave North Korea, he said that only months before the war broke out in 1950, when he was in his final year at the university, an older cousin from his mother's side of the family, a party member, told him in confidence that war was coming and all able-bodied young men would be drafted. My father was not about to fight and perhaps die for a cause he did not believe in, so he dropped everything, went back to Woldong as fast as he could, and persuaded his father to pack up and move the entire family south, taking a smuggler's ship down the east coast. But he also told me he'd been convinced long before that he couldn't live in the kind of society the country was becoming. There was the behavior of the party zealots in the university, bullying other students and fashioning themselves as an elite in a society that claimed to have no elites, and the endless series of rallies and ideology lectures they were forced to attend. But what happened to your grandfather, that's what really hit home for him."

☯

In the traditional economic system of the village, when harvest time came along, the patriarch of the family hired a broker from the local market to find out how much apples would fetch that year. Once the price was determined, the broker also arranged for the year's crop to be taken to the market and sold to the merchants. After the sale, the workers received the harvest money they depended on to carry them through the winter, the amount varying according to the year's fortune. There was no written law dictating that the patriarch had to pay them fairly in accordance with how much he made at the market, so if he decided to give them little in a profitable year, the workers had no legal means of forcing him to do otherwise. But it would never have occurred to someone like Inho's grandfather to cheat them, mainly because of his position in the community. He was neither a powerful landholder, nor an industrialist who could set wages according to whim. If he had given the workers less than they deserved, people would have found out about it, and he would have lost face as a headman and been ostracized from the social life of the village. Also, as a literate gentleman of the Confucian mode, he would have regarded it as the height of lowly behavior to exploit people in that fashion, the kind of thing a grubby city merchant does.

When the communists put the new system in place, the workers naturally thought they would make more money by dealing with the market brokers directly, or by cutting out the middleman entirely and selling the crop themselves. That situation might have come about, at least for the few years before the war, but they had not counted on the personal initiative of Comrade Dokgo. As communism was being implemented, the state took over what little industry existed at the time, rationed products manufactured from them, and enacted the land reform, but private property and the market system was maintained, especially in the larger cities. In rural areas, however, the local party officials had a great deal of discretion, especially when it came to harassing, confiscating the properties of, and, in many cases, destroying major landowning families, former Japanese collaborators, and other elements they deemed reactionary. Comrade Dokgo's ambition was to distinguish himself by turning the district under his command fully communist in record time, so it could serve as a model for others.

When harvest time came, the workers looked forward to the profits for the year, but then found out that the district officials had already set the prices for every crop. The immediate result of this policy was the collapse of the local market system, as its brokers and merchants could no longer make a profit. Without them, the workers had to take the crop to the market themselves, which was now run by officials, where they learned that they would be making significantly less money with the fixed prices—not enough, in fact, to carry them through the winter. Although officials explained to them that the People's Committee would give them whatever they lacked, they returned home dejected and worried.

"In the winter they were rationed coal, oil, and other necessities," Inho told Julie, "but they were poorer than before. They also felt humiliated, having to stand in lines to receive handouts like beggars. Within weeks, some of them were asking my grandfather to buy them out so they could move to a city and start a new life there, but he was in the same position. He was going to sell off the property of the local school since the place was closed down by the Committee, but it was confiscated with promises of a new school to be built there the following year. So the situation became tight for everyone concerned."

"What did my grandfather do?"

Inho sighed and took a large sip of water.

"He became bitter," he said. "He was terribly disappointed with the new society. He was one of the people who wanted to sell his land and leave Woldong. My grandfather explained to him that he did not have the means to buy him out, but he did not believe him. He was convinced that the family had money hidden somewhere and was holding out just to spite him. He told people that all he wanted was to move to a big city and get a job so that his son could get a decent education. When he was drunk, he would claim that my grandfather was deliberately thwarting his plan because he wanted his highborn son to be the only person in the village to attend a university."

"He must have really annoyed your grandfather."

"According to my father, he wasn't pleased with his behavior, but felt sad for him more than anything else. As the headman he was like a father to the entire community. My grandfather was only ten years older than yours, but he felt protective toward him and thought that his behavior was at least partly due to some failing on his own part."

"So what did my grandfather end up doing?" Julie asked.

"He tried to make some fast money so he could leave the village. The only way he could do that . . . well, you see, most of the brokers and merchants had left the area for the cities, but a few stayed. They bought some goods themselves and began to put together a black market network. It was small scale at first, but it grew rapidly due to the demand created by all the sudden changes. Your grandfather began by selling his leftover crop to them, then got others to sell their goods to him before passing them onto his contacts. By the following year, he was fully involved in the business and made some money. He planned on staying only after the next harvest season, when he thought he would have enough to start a new life."

"But something went wrong," Julie guessed.

"In the summer . . . my great-grandfather died. My father returned to attend the funeral. Only days after that, there was a big roundup. It turned out that Comrade Dokgo had known all about the black market. He was just waiting for the right time to swoop down on it. A high party official from Pyongyang was visiting the district. To demonstrate his zeal, he put on a big show trial of the reactionary criminals."

"My grandfather."

"He was among them. Your father . . . he was only fourteen then. His mother fainted when she heard that her husband had been arrested, so he was the one who came running to my grandfather's house. In the courtyard, he fell on his hands and knees, crying and begging him to save his father's life. 'Please tell them that I was the criminal,' he said to my grandfather. 'Please tell them that so they will take me and spare father's life. My parents can always have another son, but how will mother and sister live without father?' Although it was impossible, he was willing to sacrifice himself for his family. He was a loyal son."

Julie looked down, trembling a little.

"Are you all right?" Inho asked.

She sniffed and nodded. "Go on."

"My grandfather went to the district police station where he was being held. He wasn't allowed to see the prisoner and his pleas were answered only with curses, but a young policeman who knew him took him outside and told him that he would have better luck at the People's Committee office. He went there, saw a few officials and tried to speak for your grandfather, but he was frightened and made mistakes. He had brought some money to see if bribing someone would help the matter, but ended up giving it to the wrong official, someone unrelated to the case who listened to him, took the money and disappeared. Finally, one official got annoyed with him and yelled at him, threatening to put him in jail if he did not get out of his sight at once. He returned to the police station and begged the young policeman to let him see the prisoner. It took some hours, but he was finally sneaked into the basement where dozens of frightened men, reeking of excrement, were cramped together in tiny cells. When your grandfather saw him, he ran to the bars and cried, begging him to save his life. My grandfather, who knew that he had already failed, could only hold his hands and cry with him. As he only had a moment, he quickly handed him some food he brought with him. When the other prisoners saw that, they rushed to grab and fight over it, causing a commotion. A pair of policemen came down to see what the noise was about, beat back the prisoners with batons, then dragged my grandfather out of the police station and kicked him to the ground .

"The next day, the entire village was forced to come out and watch the outdoor trial. At the end of it, a dozen men, including your grandfather, were tied to posts and shot. His wife fainted before the rifles were fired, but your father saw it all, clinging to the hands of the man who couldn't save his father's life."

Julie cried, but only briefly and silently. She quickly wiped her eyes with her napkin and sat back.

"I know it's a lot," Inho said, feeling guilty as if he were somehow partly responsible for what had occurred five decades ago and an ocean away.

"No kidding," she replied in a far away voice.

A long, heavy moment passed before she turned to him again.

"So what happened afterward?" she asked.

"Your father, his sister, and mother were taken in by my grandfather's family. Your grandmother was in a bad way. Then her daughter, your aunt, died in the following winter from pneumonia."

"Oh God," Julie said, shaking her head in disbelief.

"After that, she withdrew from the world altogether, lying under her blankets all day. Your father nursed her and tried to revive her spirits, but it was no use. Then 1950 came along, and my father returned from Pyongyang. The family took your father and grandmother when they fled to the south, first to Seoul, then to Busan when the war began. They stayed with the family while my father served in the South Korean National Army and fought in the war. When the fighting finally came to an end, and they were preparing to move back to Seoul, your father, who had gotten a job at the docks, said he wanted to stay in Busan. My grandfather was worried about his being able to support himself and his mother alone, but respected his wishes since he seemed quite determined to make his own way. Five years later, Your father suddenly appeared at my grandfather's house in Seoul. He came to pay his respects before leaving the country. His mother had passed away the previous year and he was left by himself, so he was going to Hawaii where he had some relatives.

"My grandfather was filled with guilt at not having been able to save your grandfather and wept in front of him, as did your father. When my father came home, he talked to him about his plans, gave him what money he could scrounge up in the house and insisted that he take it despite his protests. A week later, he left the country and our family never heard from him again."

At the end of the tale, Julie and Inho sat in silence for a long time, until the restaurant began to close. After they left, Julie took Inho's hand, and they wandered through the area for a while, the dwindling crowd and the foggy lights hardly interfering with their thoughts. When the chill of the night air began to bite into them, they left in Julie's car and she drove him to the hotel. She parked the car in front and they exchanged email addresses, with promises to keep in touch and perhaps to meet in Korea if they could arrange it.

They embraced for a moment, Julie giving him a quick kiss on the cheek. Inho was about to open the car door, when she put a hand on his arm, making him stop and turn to her.

"Wait," she said. "What happened yesterday. Wow. You saved me. You get it?"

"What do you . . . "

"Your grandfather. Him feeling guilty toward my father. But you saved me."

And it was that mystery Inho was pondering some twelve hours later when the plane ascended above the pale landscape of clouds.

He thought, how does one think about a coincidence so suggestive of meaning that one is almost forced to speak of fate? But even given the specific cultural context of the story, there was no appearance of a restless spirit in the shamanistic mode, nor an intimation of metaphysical symmetry in the Buddhist manner. There was only the imperative of Confucian duty and a man's failure to fulfill it, and the Way of the Scholar does not speak of spirits or fate. When a disciple asked Master Kong about ghosts, he answered, 'How can we speak of the things of the dead when we do not know about the things of the living?' Yet he did believe in the reality of Heaven's Mandate and the power of a benevolent man to do good in the world. So, is it not possible that even an earthly obligation, given sufficient weight of guilt and regret, could reach across generations in space and time to complete itself through the occurrence of the most absurd of coincidences?

GYEONGBOK PALACE: HISTORY, CONTROVERSY, GEOMANCY

> We live amidst so many rumors. The stratum of rumors is thick and heavy. We call this history and we call it culture. It is a sad thing to live one's life as if listening to a rumor. When we are no longer satisfied with rumors and seek the place of occurrence, that is when we meet destiny.
>
> —Choe Inhun, *Gwangjang*

INTRODUCTION

What follows is partly history, partly rumor, and partly confession.

The history of Gyeongbok Palace in Seoul, the royal residence of fifteen monarchs of Korea's Joseon dynasty, will be traced from its original construction in the late fourteenth century through the cycles of destructions and reconstructions it underwent in the following five centuries. The narrative will provide the historical context for the controversy that lasted in the Korean media from 1993 to 1995 over the question of demolishing the National Museum Building, that will reveal not only a secret history of the palace, one steeped in ancient, magical beliefs, but also the problematic attitude that modern Koreans have toward the nation's past.

I have studied to become an academic historian, but this essay is not a work of scholarly history in the strict sense. I have neither burdened it with a massive list of references and notes to support its findings, nor taken on the objective voice of the historian as a recording angel. I have set out, instead, to describe my own sense of wonder and to explain why I distrust that feeling.

What follows is partly history, partly rumor, and partly confession. But every history is partly rumor and partly confession; every rumor is partly history and partly confession; and every confession is partly history and partly rumor. And I believe that it is in the rare and ineffable moments when history, rumor, and confession intermingle that the past reveals itself in its most intimate and human form.

What follows is also a dream, or perhaps the recurring nightmare of someone trying to come to terms with a traumatic event. It is a haunting as well, for what is history but the irrepressible visitations of ghosts seeking to return to life, not as human beings, but as something much more enduring.

THE PALACE OF FIFTEEN KINGS

Gyeongbok Palace lies at the northern edge of Seoul's midtown area, which is surrounded by a series of hills. The easiest way to reach the place is by taking either the third (orange) subway line, which stops right below the palace grounds, or the glistening new, fifth (purple) line to Ganghwa Gate station, but I suggest starting on Taepyeong Road near City Hall and walking northward up the street, in order to get the full effect of the view. As you approach the lofty statue of Admiral Yi Sunsin in the middle of the street, which widens out to become the perennially packed sixteen-lane Sejong Road, you will face the green peaks of Bugak Mountain. The southern gate of Ganghwa ('luminous achievement') stands below it, a solid structure of white stone topped by an elaborately decorated double-tiered roof. Walk past the statue with the Sejong Cultural Center on your left and the American Embassy complex on your right and cross the street through an underground walkway to reach the southern wall of the building. You can enter the outer grounds through Ganghwa Gate, which I recommend in order to fully appreciate the intricate and colorful designs of the roof. But you will then find your view of the rest of the palace blocked by the high scaffolding that hides the work being done to remove the remains of the recently demolished National Museum Building. You must turn to the east side of the outer grounds to reach the official entrance, where you can purchase a ticket to be admitted into the central section of the palace.

Most of the tourists will be gathered around the two largest buildings—Geunjeongjeon ('diligent rule'), an imposing wooden structure set on a vast base of stone that served as the audience hall where the kings conducted their public business, and Gyeonghoeru ('auspicious meeting'), a grand two-story pavilion, on a wide, square pond, where royal banquets were held. You have to find your way through a complex network of low roofed walls to reach other places of interest, including Sanjeongjeon ('thoughtful rule'), the king's private working quarters, which contains a famous mural of a pair of four-toed dragons; Cheonchujeon ('thousand autumns'), the hall of court scholars where the Korean writing system was invented under the direct guidance of King Sejong the Great (r. 1418—1450); Hyangwonjeon ('fragrant distance'), a dainty structure on a tiny island; and an obscure corner on the northern side of the grounds where a lone stone tablet marks the place where the body of Queen Min, the powerful wife of the penultimate monarch, Gojong (r. 1864—1907), was desecrated by Japanese assassins in 1895.

If you go to the palace expecting to see a series of sprawling, multistoried mansions and lofty fortifications in the European manner, you may be puzzled by the architecture of the place. With the exception of the audience hall and the main pavilion, all the buildings are rather small and squat, separated from one another by interconnected walls that give you a sense of being in a maze. Rulers of nations made up of flat plains tended to build high edifices that could be seen for miles around. In a hilly country like Korea, however, where flat land is precious, the most conspicuous way of exhibiting power was to occupy a great tract of open space and turn it into a place of secrets. So in imagining the grandiosity of the palace in its heyday, you must keep the horizontal plane, rather than the vertical, in mind. The palace once contained some 330 buildings, which stood over 410,000 square meters of land, and was a true labyrinth of dizzying complexity, one through which hundreds of slaves, servants, courtesans, entertainers, soldiers, eunuchs, scholars, generals, ministers, and royalty scurried in service or in pursuit of power.

THE PALACE IN KOREAN HISTORY, 1392—1963

In 1392, General Yi Seonggye completed his coup d'état of the Goryeo Kingdom by ascending the throne as the first king (r. 1392—1398) of the Joseon dynasty. The new monarch ruled from the old capital of Songdo (today's Gyeseong in North Korea) for two years, consolidating his power and negotiating with the Ming Empire of China for recognition of his rule's legitimacy. But he felt insecure living amidst the hostile noble families of the fallen kingdom, and it was also rumored that he became haunted by the ghost of Wang Geon (r. 918—943), the founder of Goryeo, after the royal family of the old dynasty was massacred in a series of bloody purges. The King resolved to move the capital to a new city and sent out numerous agents to look for an ideal place. Among the royal emissaries was the Buddhist priest Muhak (a quintessential Zen name meaning 'no knowledge'), who was knowledgeable in the art of pungsu jiri (literally, 'the principles of wind, water, and land' and the equivalent of the Chinese feng shui, sometimes translated as 'geomancy'). As Muhak was a close confidant of the King, his advice to halt the construction of a city at Sindoan, below Gyeryeong Mountain, was heeded, and a site above the Han river called Hanyang (today's Seoul, the capital of the Republic of Korea) was chosen instead. The new place was protected by a series of hills with a access route to the northeast. After further study of the area, a location below Bugak Mountain, situated in the northwestern corner, was determined to be the best place to build the royal palace.

Construction of the palace began in the tenth lunar month of 1394 and was completed in a little under a year. The building was named Gyeongbok ('great fortune') by Jeong Dojeon (1337—1398), the King's chief advisor and Confucian ideologue, who took it from the last two characters of a line in the ancient Chinese Book of Songs: 'Since you are already drunk on liquor and sated by virtue, your ten thousand years as a superior man will be blessed by a great fortune.'

The palace served as the royal residence and the center of the kingdom's administration through the reigns of the first thirteen kings of the Joseon dynasty. In 1592, the twenty-fourth year of the reign of King Seonjo, the Japanese launched a major invasion of the Korean peninsula. As the flimsy defense of the ill-prepared Joseon army collapsed before the onslaught of the two-hundred-thousand-man war machine, the royal court fled Hanyang, which fell a mere twenty days after the Japanese landed at the southern port city of Busan. The palace was set on fire and burned completely to the ground.

What tourist brochures and history textbooks may neglect to tell you is that the terrible destruction was not the work of the Japanese. After the court evacuated the city, jeered at and pelted with stones by common people who were disgusted by their nobles' cowardice and incompetence, the palace slaves sought to free themselves by setting fire to the building containing the records of their servitude. The flames spread to other structures and eventually reduced the entire place to ashes. The city was recaptured in a few months by the intervening Ming army, but the palace was left in ruins for the next 273 years, the royal residence moved to the more modest Changdeok Palace.

After the brilliant reigns of the last two great rulers of the dynasty,

King Yeongjo (r. 1724—1776) and his grandson Jeongjo (r. 1776—1800), the kingdom went into a radical decline from which it would never recover. The subsequent monarchs, who were easily-manipulated boy-kings, became mere puppets in the political struggle between the Kim clan of Andong and Jo clan of Pungyang. In 1864, twelve-year- old Prince Myeongbok (King Gojong) assumed the throne. When his father was appointed regent and given the title of Daewongun ('prince of the great house'), the former drunkard and wastrel surprised everyone by proving to be a decisive and fearful despot.

The Daewongun ruled the country as an absolute dictator for the next nine years, getting rid of anyone who stood in his way. He put a lid on the factional feuds in the court, then slammed the door on all foreigners except the Ching Chinese, ordering the military in coastal cities to fire their cannons at any foreign ships. In 1866, an American merchant vessel by the name of General Sherman was sunk on the Taedong River. In the same year, the suppression of Catholics was ordered, resulting in the slaughter of some eight thousand converts and nine French missionaries. The French sent seven warships to Ganghwa Island in response, but were driven away by a fierce counterattack. It was at this time that the country came to be known as the Hermit Kingdom.

To wrest power from the nobility and increase the prestige of the royal family, the Daewongun also embarked on his most ambitious and foolhardy project—the complete reconstruction of Gyeongbok Palace. Work began in the fourth lunar month of 1865 and took over four years to complete, employing some 36,000 workers. Against the opposition of nearly everyone in the court, he created a special tax and extorted 'voluntary offerings' from the rich to pay the colossal bills. The palace was restored in a magnificent fashion, and the court returned to it in the eleventh lunar month of 1869, but the project nearly bankrupted the kingdom and caused much resentment against the regent. When the King came of age in 1871, his wife, Queen Min, moved against her father-in-law and engineered his fall from power two years later.

While King Gojong, at the behest of his wife, ended the Daewongun's isolationist policy and opened up the nation to the rest of the world, events already well under way in East Asia would overwhelm the kingdom. In 1894, the Chinese and Japanese armies marched into Korea under the pretext of helping to put down the Donghak Rebellion. When the Japanese emerged victorious in the Sino-Japanese War of 1894-1895, Queen Min tried to counter their now dominant presence in the peninsula by making overtures to the Russians. In 1895, the Japanese ambassador Miura Goro responded by bringing in assassins who slipped into the palace at dawn on October 8, stabbed the Queen in the chest before burning her body and those of her attendants. The Japanese army subsequently occupied the palace and ousted all anti-Japanese ministers. King Gojong, fearing for his life and that of his son, fled the place with the Crown Prince on February 11 of the following year and took up residence in the Russian consulate. As the unfortunate King chose to live in Deoksu Palace when he left the consulate two years later, no reigning monarch has set foot in Gyeongbok Palace again.

Despite desperate attempts by King Gojong to maintain Korea's independence, including sending a secret envoy to the International Peace Convention in the Hague in 1907, he was forced to sign a protectorate treaty with the Japanese and to abdicate in favor of his young son Sunjong (r. 1907—1910). In 1910, Korea officially became a colony of the Japanese Empire.

In the first years of the colonial era, all but ten or so buildings of Gyeongbok Palace were torn down, the entire southern wall was destroyed, and Ganghwa Gate was removed stone by stone from the eastern wall. In 1912, a German architect by the name of Georg de Lalande, who was residing in Tokyo, was hired to design the Japanese Government-General Building in Korea. The construction of the massive five-story, neo-Renaissance style, granite structure began in

June 1916 and was completed in October 1926. The complex was erected on the front part of the palace grounds, completely eclipsing what remained of the palace.

The Japanese left the country after their defeat in World War II, and the Republic of Korea was inaugurated in 1948. While there was some discussion of tearing down the former Government-General Building, President Rhee Syngman himself favoring the idea, the cost of the work proved too great for the impoverished nation. Instead it was used as the Government Building of the Korean republic until 1983, when it was converted into the National Museum. Reconstruction and renovation of Gyeongbok Palace began in 1963, when Ganghwa Gate was moved back to its original location.

THE CONTROVERSY, 1993—1995

I first became interested in the history of Gyeongbok Palace because of the discussions in the Korean media from 1993 to 1995 over the question of demolishing the National Museum Building, which used to be the Government Building, which used to be the Government-General Building of the Japanese Empire. In August of 1993, President Kim Youngsam announced that the structure, as a legacy of the colonial era, would be destroyed in 1995, the fiftieth anniversary of Korea's liberation from the Japanese and the six-hundredth anniversary of the completion of the original palace. The proposal was met with wide approval by the public, but it immediately set off a bitter two-year controversy over the fate of the building.

The pro-demolitionists argued that, as Korea now possessed the tenth largest economy in the world as well as a truly democratic political system which had brought to power the first civilian president in decades, it was high time the country got rid of this remnant from the time of subjugation. The building that had been erected in front of the palace of the old kings to symbolize Japanese imperial dominance should be erased, they argued, in order to mark Korea's transcendence from the great trials of the past and its achievement of prosperity and freedom.

The preservationists, however, thought that it was the height of jingoistic stupidity and a gross waste of the taxpayers' money to destroy a perfectly good building that also served as a fine museum. They pointed out that the estimated coast would be 5 billion won (around $6 million at the time) for the demolition work alone, plus some 25 billion won (around $30 million) for the construction of a building to house the museum's artifacts. In addition, it would require some 180 billion won (over $210 million) to clean up and renovate Gyeongbok Palace. A proposal to move the building block by block to a different location was rejected outright when the estimated cost turned out to be astronomical. The preservationists questioned what real purpose it served to destroy the building. Isn't it time the nation moved on from its obsession with the humiliation of half a century ago? If the building is demolished, Japan remains the same, but Korea will have squandered over 200 billion won and ended up with one less place to put its national treasures. To them, it was a simple matter of practical reason versus irrational nationalism.

Historians were also bitterly divided over the issue. The pro-demolitionists among them pointed out that the Japanese were unwilling, to this day, to face up to the crimes they had committed during the imperial era. This was exemplified by their refusal to make a proper apology and award reparations to the surviving Korean women who had been forced into sexual slavery (the so-called comfort women) during World War II; the success of Japanese books detailing how ungrateful Koreans are for all the wonderful things that were done for their country as a Japanese colony; the movement by right-wing groups to claim Dok Island; and the continued use of outdated history textbooks with glaring inaccuracies about both early and modern Korea. We need to make a strong and spectacular statement of outrage, they argued, by destroying that most prominent remainder of Japanese presence on the peninsula, and invite foreign journalists to witness the event.

But preservationist historians pointed out that while the building was erected by the Japanese, it also played an important part in the history of the Korean republic, having served as the center of government administration for most of the nation's history. During a lively television debate on the issue, one historian brought in an enlargement of the famous 1948 photograph of President Rhee Syngman taking the oath of office in front of the structure, before a great crowd of people, and below the national flag. The building is an integral part of our history now, the historian asserted, and to destroy it is to destroy a part of our own heritage. Another historian said that we ought to preserve the building precisely because it is an odious reminder of the colonial era—not only will its presence keep us from forgetting what was done to us, it will also provide a lesson in what can happen if we become weak enough to lose our independence. He went on to say that you do not tear down the Pyramids because slave labor was used to build them, nor do you destroy Auschwitz because horrible things were done there. What these monuments have to teach us is far too important.

As I followed the discussions closely, I found most interesting and puzzling at the same time, the frequent mention of ideas from pungsu jiri (geomancy). As I knew little about the ancient art, I was bewildered by the great passion with which some of the participants in the debates discussed the National Museum Building and Gyeongbok Palace in geomantic terms. What also struck me was the fact that their magical ideas were taken seriously by the media and so could not be dismissed as the strange ramblings of a few eccentrics. I knew that geomancy was no mere superstition for many Koreans since it is still a common practice to hire a geomancer to look over the land one is thinking of purchasing or building on. An MIT-educated engineer once told me that his first computer parts manufacturing business had failed because the factory was built on a geomantically unsound place, and I recently found out that my late grandfather, a devout Christian and a professor of geography no less, had consulted a geomancer when looking for a suitable gravesite for himself and his wife.

In considering the various debates over the controversy, I had no problem understanding the argument of national pride, of practical economics, of historical outrage, and of historical preservation. But it was difficult for me, with my Western education, to take the geomancy argument seriously. My skepticism was reinforced by recent reports in the media of 'geomantic crimes' and 'geomantic frauds.' Some people had secretly buried the bodies of their parents on 'auspicious' land that belonged to someone else, hoping to generate great fortune through the act, while unscrupulous geomancers received bribes from real-estate agents to declare certain property propitious in order to increase its value. Other geomancers had declared the gravesite of the parents of President Park Chunghee to be auspicious since the family had produced a ruler of the nation, but when Park was assassinated in 1979, the land was declared to be unlucky. The same thing happened with the gravesites of the parents of Presidents Chun Doohwan and Roh Taewoo, which were declared propitious when the leaders were in power, but reassessed as unlucky when both went to jail in 1996 for corruption. And I understand the gravesite of the parents of the current president, Kim Daejung, is supposed to be lucky now and is visited by a steady stream of tourists.

Nevertheless, I felt that I needed to learn more about pungsu jiri in order to comprehend the passions involved. What I found was not only a complex system of thought with a rich and fascinating tradition, but also a secret history of the places at the heart of the controversy.

THE SECRET HISTORY OF GEOMANCY

Modern Western physiology regards the human body basically as a machine consisting of discrete parts, each with a specific function in maintaining the life of the organism. When a person falls ill, the question to ask is, which part has broken down or is not working properly? Once the source of the malfunction is identified, it is isolated and repaired so that it may once again perform its role in the mechanical system.

Traditional East Asian medicine, on the other hand, sees the body as a vessel through which gi (vital energy) flows, animating the corporeal mass. The gi travels through points of vital concentration, called hyeol, which are distributed all over the body. At each of these points, the energy accumulates so that its speed, temperature, and quantity can be regulated. Within this system of medicine, an illness is defined as an imbalance or disharmony in the flow of the gi which is caused by a leakage, blockage, or weakening along its path and which may have an internal or external cause. Acupuncture manipulates these hyeol points in order to correct the flow or to reroute it to places where it is needed the most. Since gi paths are all interconnected, a doctor may treat, say, stomach pain by putting needles in such disparate places as the shoulder, tips of fingers, and back of the neck in order to restore harmony. Of course, it would be of no use for me to insist at this point that this actually works, especially for chronic pain and psychosomatic disorders that Western medicine can do little about, since few in the West are convinced until they try it. But the effectiveness of such treatment does not necessarily prove the general physiological ideas of East Asian medicine, just as the efficacy of Western science does not validate its world view.

The ancient Chinese art of feng shui is based on exactly the same model, but applied to the natural environment. Gi moves through the living organism of the earth by means of wind, water, and mountain ranges. When it flows in a harmonious and regular manner, the weather is mild and good for farming, water and air are clear, and all creatures thrive. When it is blocked or dissipated by an alteration in the landscape, a structure erected in the wrong place, for example, the weather turns nasty, disasters like floods and earthquakes occur constantly, and diseases wreak havoc on the inhabitants. A geomancer is both a doctor of the environment, diagnosing the cause of natural calamities and finding the remedies, and an assessor who determines the geomantic health and value of the land.

One of the most important concepts in geomancy is that of myeongdang (literally, a 'radiant place'). The ultimate philosopher's stone of geomancers, myeongdang is the geomantic equivalent of a hyeol—a place where a strong flow of gi accumulates and is warmed and cooled simultaneously by an optimal conjunction of geographical features. Such a place usually has a circular mountain range, which brings in the gi, and is bordered by a river that cools the vital energy down before sending it on.

When you examine the illustrations of different myeongdang types in geomantic treatises, you notice that the concept makes perfect geographical sense as well. A settlement built in such a location would not only be protected by the mountains, but would also be right next to a water source. Even though it expresses itself in the terminology of magic, geomancy is one of the most ancient forms of a comprehensive science of environmental and urban planning. And in a small, mountainous nation like Korea, where there is limited space to build settlements, it was an essential art.

The more utilitarian aspects of geomancy, however, went into decline in both Joseon dynasty Korea and Ming dynasty China. A minor aspect of the art, the concept of generating good fortune by burying one's parents at a myeongdang, eventually emerged as its main tenant. Geomancers became agents of the rich and the powerful who hired them to look for such a place, a practice that continues to this day. In the nineteenth century, the great populist poet Kim Sakgat (1807—1863), in one of his many poems satirizing the greed of the wealthy and the incompetence of scholars, condemned the geomancers as well:

All geomancers are frauds.
Tongues wagging, busily pointing North and South.
If there really is a radiant place in those mountains,
Why did you not bury your own father there?

Feng shui comes largely out of Daoist thought as elements of it can be found in the sayings of the first masters Laozi (circa sixth century BCE) and Chuangzi (circa third century BCE). It was introduced into Korea during the era of the Unified Silla Kingdom (669—935 CE), with the first great master of the art, the Buddhist priest Doseon, emerging in the ninth century. By the time the Goryeo dynasty was founded in 918, geomancy was regarded as a legitimate scholarly subject and was taught at major learning institutions. It never became a core subject of civil-service examinations, but the more ambitious practitioners of the art could take the government's so-called miscellaneous examinations. This allowed them to enter the ranks of technical scholars, with the hope of one day becoming the court geomancer, who was consulted on matters concerning building and settlement sites, as well as the all-important place for a royal grave.

The strangest episode in Korean history involving geomancy occurred in the early twelfth century, during the reign of the Goryeo monarch Injong (r.1122—1146). The kingdom was in crisis at the time as a major rebellion was barely suppressed, the royal palace at Songdo was completely destroyed by fire during the conflict, and the Ruzhen Jin state of Northern China began exerting military pressure on the peninsula. Two of the King's high ministers, Bek Suhan and Jeong Jisang, and a Buddhist priest by the name of Myocheong, who was reputed to be a powerful geomancer, urged the King to move the capital to their native city of Seokyeong (today's Pyongyang, the capital of North Korea). The men argued that the misfortunes of the kingdom were due to the weakening of gi in Songdo. Myocheong went so far as to claim that the Seokyeong site he had in mind for the new royal residence was such a potent myeongdang that moving the court there would not only cause all the problems of the kingdom to disappear, but also prompt the Jin Empire to surrender of its own accord and make Injong the master of thirty-six nations. The King was persuaded, and a palace was built there and completed in 1129. But even as the court prepared to make the journey from Songdo, the entire country was shaken by a series of terrible natural disasters. When an enormous lightening bolt struck just outside the newly built residence, it was universally regarded as a bad omen and the move was canceled. Most historians interpret the episode as an attempt by the Seokyeong men to use geomancy to increase the prestige of their hometown and thus their own status, but that does not wholly explain what occurred next. Myocheong, apparently believing every word of his outlandish claims about the power of the place, raised a ragtag band of armed men and occupied the city in 1135, declaring himself king. He strutted around for a few weeks, claiming to be a ruler destined to conquer the world, and bullied the local people until they got fed up with him and arrested him and his band. They were all subsequently executed for treason.

But farcical events of this nature were not the only results of geomantic ideas on the nation's history. If you go up to the observation tower on Nam Mountain and look down on the central part of the great chaotic sprawl that is today's Seoul, you will see that the place is a textbook case of a myeongdang—a network of hills surrounding it to the north and the Han River bordering it to the south. To fully understand the configuration, we must return to 1394, when the first king of the Joseon dynasty chose the site for his new capital and the royal residence.

The tract of land below Bugak Mountain was chosen for the palace because court geomancers determined that it was a hyeol upon which an enormous amount of gi poured down like a great waterfall from the heights. They believed that the energy would accumulate at the palace before spreading out across the land, like the benevolent rule of the king. They also found the place to be propitious since the mountain was in the shape of the Chinese character 'dae' ('great'). It was essential, however, to keep the area in front of the place clear in order to facilitate the flow of gi.

During the colonial era, the Japanese tried to destroy Korea in many ways, from the policy of slow eradication of the Korean language and culture, the destruction of important cultural artifacts, the rewriting of history, the outright massacres, the killing of people in concentration camps through starvation and forced labor, the medical experiments on live subjects, to the forced prostitution of nearly 200,000 women. But the most bizarre was through the use of geomancy.

For decades after liberation in 1945, there were stories that the Japanese had brought their own geomancers to Korea to determine where all the major hyeol were. The colonial authority had then ordered enormous iron spikes to be driven through those points in order to cut off the flow of gi, thus destroying all the myeongdang in the land and sapping the life from the nation, much like deliberately putting acupuncture needles in the wrong points of a body to harm it. The idea was so fantastic that the only people who took it seriously were aging geomancers who had lived during the colonial era and who claimed to have gone to the sites and seen the spikes buried in the ground. I myself thought these were ludicrous anti-Japanese rumors.

In the spring of 1995, all of Korea watched television open-mouthed as investigative reporters followed the old geomancers to some of these locations and, with the help of heavy machinery, began pulling out one iron spike after another, some of them clearly marked with Japanese characters. The geomancers claimed that through the years they had removed approximately 150 spikes on their own accord, out of some 1,000 they thought buried throughout the country. A subsequent government investigation, however, managed to locate and remove only twenty more.

It was then asserted that the Government-General Building in front of Gyeongbok Palace was the greatest gi-destroyer of them all because it featured an enormous iron dome, which supposedly blocked the energy flowing down from Bugak Mountain. Those who argued for the demolition of the building also pointed out the following. The building, when seen from above, looked like the Chinese character for 'day' – 'nip' in Japanese. Down the street was the rather oddly shaped City Hall, also built by the Japanese, which, seen from above, looked like the character for 'origin' – 'pon' in Japanese. By combining the character formed by Bugak Mountain with these, you have the three characters for 'Great Japan (Nippon),' smack in the heart of Seoul! In addition, geomancers claimed that two other major buildings erected by the Japanese, the Seoul Railway Station and the zoo and botanical garden at Changgyeong Palace, were also strategically placed to disrupt the flow of gi through the city.

I believe it was the discovery of the iron spikes that finally allowed the pro-demolitionists to win. During the National Liberation Day celebration at the palace on August 15, 1995, the iron dome was torn off the former Government-General Building amidst thunderous applause. On November 13 of the next year, at five o'clock in the afternoon, dynamite was set off at its granite base, and the entire structure collapsed in a cloud of gray dust. A few weeks later, after most of the debris was removed, a construction crew working in the basement discovered more spikes buried in the ground.

There were some nine thousand of them.

THE DRAGON IN THE POND

For some blessed countries, history is something that happened long ago and far away. For others, the present is full of the past, sometimes as a great burden that prevents forward movement and other times as a great storm that sweeps everything up and takes it to some unknown place in the future. A historian living in a fortunate country may complain of the public's lack of interest in the past, but it should be realized that the people to whom history matters the most are those of troubled lands, where the tempest of events is still raging. The passion that is aroused in discussions of the past by the people of Bosnia, Palestine, or Northern Ireland cannot be matched in similar discussions by those of, say, Canada or Sweden. That is why I find the Korean obsession with history both fascinating and sad.

I am not a historian of Korea. Although I am Korean and know the culture and language intimately, I lived in the country for only eight years as a child, returning in 1995 to fulfill my compulsory military duty. While it would be an exaggeration to call myself an outsider, I cannot help always feeling slightly removed. Even as I make my way through Seoul, conversing with people, acting in the proper manner, following the correct rituals of everyday life, I have a sense of playing a part like an actor. For nearly two decades I grew up away from my native land, educating myself in Western history, philosophy, and literature, learning to have greater command of the English language, developing close relationships with Americans, and attending graduate school in the United States to become a historian of modern Europe. I remember as an undergraduate reading Dostoyevsky's *The Possessed* and wincing at Shatov's passionate words:

> Rest assured that those who cease to understand the people of their own country and lose contact with them also lose the faith of their forefathers and become godless or indifferent. Yes, yes, it always proves true: that's why you and the lot of us today are either despicable atheists or indifferent, vicious human muck.

Then I returned to the country and became a part of the Army of the Republic of Korea, the toughest institution I have ever been a part of. I was turned into a soldier and sent to a hellhole near the Demilitarized Zone because I owed it to my country to defend it against communism, six years after the fall of the Berlin Wall and the dissolution of the Soviet Union and the Warsaw Pact. Kim Ilsung, the founder and long-time dictator of North Korea, had died suddenly the year before, and the military situation on the peninsula was still tense. As the economy of the North was deteriorating rapidly, some speculated that the leadership of the country would decide to invade the South before it became worse. In 1996, when a malfunctioning North Korean submarine was discovered off the South's east coast and most of its crew found dead, the entire Army of the Republic of Korea went on full alert. While reconnaissance units based in Gangwon Province searched for the six infiltrators who had been aboard the submarine, the company I was stationed with went on standby and had to wait in battle-ready condition. Our platoon commander even told us to write a letter to our parents because troop movements in the North suggested that we might be at war in a few days. I saw some of the toughest men in the unit break down and weep at the announcement, while others lost control of their bladders. The experience of being a part of history rather than a scholar of it proved traumatic enough, so I resolved to do my best to avoid it for the rest of my life.

A few months after I was promoted to corporal and sent home on leave, I watched the destruction of the National Museum Building on television. As I had closely followed the debates during the controversy, I had strong but ambivalent feelings about the dramatic conclusion. It was only after I was finally discharged from the army in the summer of 1997 that I considered writing about the event. In order to familiarize myself with its historical background, I visited Gyeongbok Palace several times, talked with professors and graduate students at Seoul National University, and spent many hours at the National Library delving into ancient texts.

After I finished my research and wrote up a preliminary draft of this essay, I returned to the palace and walked around the grounds for a whole afternoon before going home and reading over my work. There were many aspects of the early version that dissatisfied me, but the most glaring fault seemed to be its tone. While I presented every interesting discovery I had made and every fascinating fact I had unearthed, I marveled at the strangeness and incomprehensibility of it all, as if I were an old archaeologist in a pith helmet walking through an Egyptian maze and exclaiming 'ooh!' and 'aah!' at every turn. When I returned to my country and re-immersed myself in its culture, what struck me most was the constant presence of seemingly contradictory elements.

If you walk around the teeming streets if Seoul, you will find that it looks, sounds, and smells like a modern metropolis, but you don't have to delve too deeply to find a second city, one built on a firm belief in the efficacy of geomancy, shamanistic rituals, and ancestor worship, the existence of ghosts, demons, and natural deities, and the manifestation of the Heaven's Mandate in history. I regarded the persistence of geomantic beliefs in contemporary Korea and their involvement in the debates over the demolition of the National Museum Building as more examples of contradictions inherent in the modern Korean condition. In the last months of finishing this essay, however, as I found myself going deeper into the cultural matrix, I came to question whether that was the proper way to present the issues involved. It even occurred to me that since I was writing for an English-language audience, I might have done some 'orientalizing' for the benefit of Western readers.

When the twentieth century began, Korea was still a feudal country ruled by royalty and a small landowning elite. Starting in 1910, the nation was exploited for thirty-five years by a hostile power bent on eradicating its identity. When those imperials left, two other imperial powers divided Korea, a country that had been a single nation since 985 CE. A terrible war followed during which, with the help of foreign armies and their modern weaponry, we slaughtered each other for three years, razing virtually the entire country in the process. Since then, one half of the country, through nearly forty years of absolutist rule by military dictators, developed a vibrant capitalist economy and a fully democratic political system, while the other half has remained one of the most repressive and xenophobic nations in the world. Despite the recent economic downturn in the region, the Republic of Korea is still a leading exporter of manufactured goods, and its living standards are on the level of advanced developing nations. In the North, masses of people are dying of starvation even as the Stalinist regime, one of the last in the world, continues to spend a third of its meager budget on the military.

Given the peninsula's historical legacy and the daily possibility of being swept into yet another terrible disaster, the elements in Korea's culture that I have described are not incongruous at all, but necessary, the result of living in two worlds at the same time while trying to keep from being driven mad by history. In holding on to traditional ideas and magical beliefs that may seem out of place today, Korea is trying to overcome all that happened to it in this century and to heal the wounds inflicted by modernity. In the face of the irresistible necromancy of history, which does not recognize human time, the victims of the past must use their oldest talismans to ward off the present's darkest magic.

In the last months of 1997, as I was beginning to ponder the history of Gyeongbok Palace, the Republic of Korea went into major economic crisis as the value of the stock market and the currency plummeted. Conditions continued to deteriorate such that in 1998 the country found itself in the humiliating position of having to go to the International Monetary Fund (IMF) for immediate loans. Meanwhile, major companies and small businesses alike began to go bankrupt and unemployment reached a record high. Despite the obvious fact that the crisis was brought on mainly through over-expansion by the larger corporations and the granting of ill-advised loans by government-owned banks with unsound policies, the media abounded with all kinds of conspiracy theories on a nefarious few in the shadows, usually foreigners, who engineered the whole thing in order to cripple the nation. Last time I was at the vast Kyobo Bookstore, just down the street from Gyeongbok Palace, I counted no less than twelve books advancing such ideas.

There was also a newspaper report that connected the economic crisis with a dragon that appeared at the palace. On November 14, 1997, it was announced that while workers were cleaning the pond around Gyeonghoeru Pavilion, they found in the water a magnificent dragon sculpture made of copper that was 146.5 cm in length and 66.5 kg in weight. A remarkably well-preserved work, the creature featured an extended tongue, a protruding mustache, and a cheerful expression. After an investigation by historians, the creature was declared to be one of two dragons that had been placed in the pond during the Daewongun's reconstruction of the palace, probably in 1867. In the third lunar month of that year, a major fire on the construction site had destroyed many of the wooden structures being put up, a disaster that had set back the date of completion by almost a year and had caused further hardship for the people. In East Asian mythology, dragons have power over the watery element, so the pieces were put in the pond as a part of a shamanist ritual to ward off more fires.

When it was announced that the dragon would be removed from the palace and displayed in a museum, more than a few shamans and soothsayers claimed that would bring misfortune to the nation. It was shortly after this that the economic crisis began in earnest, and all the mystics screamed 'I told you so!' in the media. On February 25, 1998, when the loan negotiation with the IMF was about to begin, Gyeonghoeru Pavilion was the site of an elaborate ceremony during which an exact replica of the dragon was placed in the pond by four men dressed in the traditional garb of palace servants. The IMF subsequently agreed to make the loans under conditions favorable to South Korea, and the currency, which had fallen in value from around 800 won to the US dollar to over 2,000 in less than three months, steadied at around 1,300.

☯

Before I began writing this final version of the essay, I paid one last visit to Gyeongbok Palace. I went there primarily to appreciate the view, now that the National Museum Building was gone, the first time I went somewhere to witness the absence of something. As I stood where Sejong Road begins and gazed at the panorama, the shimmering green heights of Bugak Mountain spread out like a great umbrella above the stolid Ganghwa Gate, I had to admit that the effect was magnificent.

I believe that acupuncture works, but I do not know if gi and hyeol exist. I believe that geomancy was an attempt by ancient East Asians to develop a science of environmental and urban planning, but I do not know if there is such a thing as geomantic gi or a myeongdang. I do not believe in fate or prophecy, but it frightens me that the famous old shaman one of my aunts dragged me to told me that I was destined to live in many nations, spend my life writing and teaching, and experience a major setback in my late twenties (all true), but also that the achievement of great success at a still young age would mean little to me as the loss of my beloved at the same time would cause me to forswear love and dedicate myself to art for the rest of my life.

I believe that the Korean obsession with history is the product of a sense of victimization from the calamities of the modern period. I believe that Japan should face up to its actions during the imperial era at last and make a sincere apology and proper reparations to the surviving comfort women. I could not be farther from a nationalist, and I believe that all things historical, good and bad, ought to be preserved. But as I stood before that grand view and its supposed gi flowing down to me like a great river, I could very well understand the point of demolishing the building.

Perhaps I also live in two worlds at the same time, to prevent myself from bring driven mad by history.

Seoul, 1998

THE AUTHOR

Minsoo Kang was born in 1967 and has lived in Korea, Austria, New Zealand, Brunei, Iran, Germany, and other countries for shorter periods. He served in the army of the Republic of Korea, and received his Ph.D. in European History from the University of California, Los Angeles. He is currently an assistant professor at the history department of the University of Missouri, St. Louis. His reviews and essays have appeared in *The American Historical Review*, *Manoa*, *The Times Literary Supplement*, *Rethinking History*, *Comitatus,* and two anthologies, while his short stories have been published in *Lady Churchill's Rosebud Wristlet.* He is currently working on a history book on the automaton as a cultural and intellectual symbol in the Western imagination, and putting final touches on a literary novel set in contemporary Korea.

Lightning Source UK Ltd.
Milton Keynes UK
UKOW04f1831240913

217870UK00001B/92/A

9 780809 557967